EDWARD MYERS

CLIMB OR DIE

EDWARD MYERS

CLIMB OR DIE

HYPERION BOOKS FOR CHILDREN
NEW YORK

To Walt, Paige,
Glenn, Chris, and Alison

Text © 1994 by Edward Myers.
All rights reserved. No part of this book may be used or reproduced
in any manner whatsoever without written permission
from the publisher.
Printed in the United States of America.
For information address Hyperion Books for Children,
114 Fifth Avenue, New York, New York 10011.

3   5   7   9   10   8   6   4   2

Library of Congress Cataloging-in-Publication Data

Myers, Edward. Climb or die/Edward Myers—1st ed.
p.   cm.
Summary: After a car accident in a snowy Colorado pass seriously
injures their parents, athletic fourteen-year-old Danielle and her
brainy younger brother, Jake, must scale a mountain to find help.
ISBN 0-7868-0026-7 (trade)
[1. Survival—Fiction.   2. Mountaineering—Fiction.   3. Brothers
and sisters—Fiction.   4. Colorado—Fiction.]   I. Title.
PZ7.M98255C1   1994
[Fic]—dc20 93-44861 CIP AC

Also by Edward Myers

The Mountain Made of Light
Fire and Ice
The Summit

ONE

▲

SNOW.

Danielle Darcy couldn't believe it, but what she saw on the car's windshield was snow. Not rain, not even sleet—*snow*. One moment she'd been watching the mountian scenery rush by: a brown-gray cliff on the right, a pine-covered valley on the left. The next moment everything disappeared. All she saw now was a swirl of grainy white.

"Cool!" exclaimed Danielle's thirteen-year-old brother, Jake. Sitting behind her with the family dog in the Blazer's cargo area, Jake moved around back there trying to peer out one of the windows.

Danielle, who was fourteen, couldn't have cared less what her brother thought. All she could think about was the snow. She couldn't believe how dark everything looked outside. She glanced at her watch. Four-thirty. It wouldn't be dusk for another two and a half hours, yet suddenly the whole world had gone dim.

Dad switched on the windshield wipers, then the headlights. In the beams Danielle could see so many snowflakes rush at her that the sight made her dizzy.

Leaning forward to look out, Mom asked Dad, "So what's all this?"

"Probably just a squall," Dad said. Danielle wondered what a squall was but didn't ask. She wasn't sure she wanted to know. On the other hand, Dad didn't sound too worried. He just kept driving, though by now he'd slowed down from highway speeds to about thirty miles per hour. A few cars passed the Darcys' Blazer, but others were going slower than Danielle and her family. Two or three cars had even pulled off the interstate.

"It's too early for anything but flurries," Mom said. "If you ask me, October's too early for snow of *any* kind."

"That's not true," Jake said suddenly. "Not in Colorado. Jonathan told me the Rockies get snowfall off and on even in the summertime. It's part of the alpine climate."

Danielle wasn't interested in hearing her brother's lecture, but she decided not to interrupt. She was in no mood to argue with him. She was in no mood to be with her family at all.

They drove a while longer. The only sound was the hiss-scrape, hiss-scrape of the wipers on the glass. Danielle was amazed at how fast the snow coated the windshield. Even right after the wipers swept over the glass, she could barely see outside. Now and then she caught a glimpse of the cliff on her right—big angular rocks—but there was no view on the left. Even the headlights of the oncoming cars were reduced to faint yellow disks.

Danielle didn't mind snow. Under the right circumstances—like maybe the upcoming ski season—snow would be wonderful. What she'd seen of Rocky Mountain weather that summer, during the two-week Mountain Mastery course Danielle had taken, had thrilled her. Colorado weather was wild: the clearest, bluest sky she'd ever seen, then sudden clouds and rainshowers, then blue sky again, sometimes all in less than thirty minutes. No doubt the Colorado winter would be wild, too. And also fun? Danielle thought so. In fact, winter was one of the main reasons she felt glad her family had moved to Denver. Still, this wasn't winter. This was barely autumn. "Isn't this just *great*," Danielle muttered, feeling grumpier and grumpier.

"I don't like it any better than you do," Dad replied from the driver's seat.

"I want this to be over," she said.

"Well, so do I."

Danielle started to worry that they might rear-end a car ahead of them before Dad even saw it there. Then what? Would they all be killed? Or would they end up standing outside in the snow half the night waiting for the tow truck to rescue them?

She didn't intend to speak, but just then Danielle heard herself say, "This is getting tedious."

"I'll second the motion," Jake said.

"Would you two ease up a little?" Dad said. "This is reality. This isn't TV. We can't just change channels."

Danielle reached forward in the dim light as if holding a remote control gadget. She pointed it at Dad and pressed an imaginary POWER OFF button.

"So what do we do?" Mom asked. Her voice sounded calm, but Danielle could tell she was worried. Mom's face showed no emotion. That was unusual. Her features resembled Jake's more than Danielle's: blue eyes, small nose, and light-hued skin with a few freckles. Like her son, Mom often looked serious, though she had a good sense of fun, and the corners of her mouth sometimes trembled a bit if she tried to hide her smile. Right now Danielle couldn't quite be sure what Mom was thinking, but something clearly bothered her.

"This can't keep up," Dad told Mom.

"If anything," Mom replied, "it's getting worse."

"Look, it's October eighth," Dad went on. "How

long can a storm like this go on before it fizzles out?"

Jake said, "Last year Denver had eight inches of snow on September tenth. Jonathan told me that. School got canceled for two whole days."

"He's got a point," Mom said. "We're not in New Jersey now. We don't really know what we're getting into, do we?"

Dad's only answer was to switch on the radio. At first there was just a lot of static. Then, after some bits of music, a voice came on: "—and a travel advisory for all high country roads, especially those in Routt, Jackson, Grand, Boulder, Eagle, Summit, Gilpin, and Park counties—" Dad switched off the radio.

"Well?" Mom asked.

"Well what?"

"I think we ought to turn back."

Dad said nothing for a while. Since Danielle was sitting right behind him, she couldn't see his face. Then she caught a glimpse of Dad's eyes reflected in the rearview mirror: dark brown eyes, just like Danielle's. Those eyes told her something, but she didn't know what it was. Then Dad said, "I think we need some time at the cabin."

"Fine—I agree," Mom said. "But is it really wise—"

"Jeannine, we're halfway there already."

"But just *look* at it!"

"I know," Dad told her. His voice sounded gloomy. "I know."

Danielle looked out the window and wondered if anything was out there at all. She could feel the car moving but couldn't see where it was or where it was going. All she saw was a zillion snowflakes billowing around her.

The whole world had turned to snow.

TWO

▲

WHAT'S GOING ON? JAKE DARCY wondered. He didn't know. It bothered him that his parents didn't know, either. For all he could tell, the whole family might as well have been lost in space. The view Jake saw as the car plowed through the storm was just like what an intergalactic traveler in a sci-fi movie would see when his spacecraft goes into warp speed: an infinity of bright specks rushing at him.

For a while the Darcys continued upward at about twenty miles per hour, the red taillights of a car ahead just barely visible in the storm. Then that car's right turn signal started blinking, and the driver pulled over. Jake saw other cars pulling over, too. His family's car passed a whole lot of them. His mom, dad, and sister all stared out the windows at the line of cars as they drove by. Even Flash, the Darcys' beagle, stared out the window.

"This highway's practically a parking lot," Dad said.

Mom didn't answer him. She turned on the radio.

"—deteriorating weather conditions," said the announcer. "The Colorado State Patrol has now closed the following passes: Gore, Millner, Vail, Fremont, Hoosier—"

Dad switched the radio off again.

"Why did you do that?" Mom asked.

"If we're going to spend time at the cabin," he said, "let's just get there."

"Phil, I don't think this is a good idea."

Danielle said, "Would you guys just make up your minds?"

Jake turned and settled back into the cargo area. On the left was a toolbox, a coil of towrope, and other items of Dad's work gear. On the right were two boxes of quilts and cold-weather clothes that the family had brought along, intending to leave them at their mountain house for use that coming winter. Wedged there between the two piles of stuff, Jake felt as cozy as possible under the circumstances. Having Flash beside him helped: the dog eased onto Jake's lap and nuzzled against him for comfort.

Mom switched on the radio.

"—and has restricted all nonessential traffic on Interstate 70 above Millertown."

"What highway are we on?" Mom asked.

Dad didn't answer.

Jake said, "I-70." He twisted around to see his parents' reactions.

Mom reached forward, opened the glove compartment, and rummaged around till she found a Colorado map. She switched on the overhead light. "Anybody know where we are?"

"I don't believe this," Danielle said.

"A sign back there said Bedell," Jake told them.

From the front passenger seat his mother said, "Bedell, Bedell, Bedell . . ."

Jake glanced over at Danielle. His sister glanced back, then turned away, looking disgusted.

"Don't look at *me* like that," Jake said. "You're the one who wanted to go hiking so bad."

Danielle didn't answer him. She shook her head.

Jake turned to Flash for sympathy. Just because Danielle is fourteen, Jake told himself, she thinks she knows everything. Gazing down at Flash, Jake could tell that the dog understood how he felt. Yet Flash looked uneasy, too, as if starting to wonder what these humans had gotten him into.

"Here we are," Mom said. "Bedell. We're right down the road from Millertown."

Dad just kept driving.

"Phil, they've closed the interstate above Millertown."

"I know that."

"We'd better turn around," Mom told him. "They said all nonessential traffic—"

"Look," Dad said, sounding annoyed, "I'd call us essential. I'd call this trip essential. I'd call getting to the cabin pretty damn essential—" He cut himself short. "Sorry."

Jake sat there listening. The car was quieter than it would have been otherwise, for the snow on the highway muffled its noise. The windshield wipers made the only loud sound, an odd squeak as the blades went back and forth: Sorry . . . Sorry . . . Sorry . . . Sorry . . .

Jake knew that his father was under a lot of pressure at work. Mom was, too. Dad was a construction foreman for a petrochemical company in Denver; Mom was a marketing executive at a department store. Both of them were adjusting to their new jobs. Dad seemed particularly tense about his work. Jake didn't understand what the petrochemical company did—something about extracting oil from rocks—but he knew that his dad spent a lot of time in the Colorado mountains helping the company's crews at their field sites. Unfortunately, it now appeared that the mining and extracting processes might not be profitable. If things didn't work out, Dad would lose his job.

Sorry, said the windshield wipers. Sorry . . . Sorry . . . Sorry . . . Sorry . . .

12

At this point Dad turned off the interstate, drove up an exit ramp, stopped at a stop sign, and turned left. The Darcys' Blazer drove over a bridge spanning the highway.

"What are you doing?" Mom asked, sounding more puzzled than alarmed.

"Taking a shortcut."

Jake expected his mother to say something more—to argue with Dad again—but she didn't. In some ways her silence scared Jake more than if she'd hollered, screamed, or told Dad to stop.

Suddenly they were in a forest. Jake could see faint vertical lines that must have been trees, but otherwise the car's headlights showed nothing but the swirling snow. When he looked back, more snow billowed in the Blazer's wake.

"Joe Blakely showed me this shortcut," Dad went on. "It connects I-70 with U.S. 285. We took it a few weeks ago."

Slumped in her seat, Danielle forced herself upright to have a better look ahead.

"If we can get over to 285," Dad said, "then it's only another thirty-five miles or so to the cabin."

"What do you mean, *if?*" Mom asked.

"Not if—*when.*"

"Phil, this is nuts."

"Trust me."

"I can't even see the road."

"I don't think it'll be a problem. It's an old mining road. If the miners could get up this in their horse-drawn carts, we can surely make it in a Blazer."

Jake leaned forward to look past his dad. The speedometer read about twenty miles per hour. The odometer read 16,401. The gas gauge read half full. He wasn't sure what difference any of this made, but it reassured him to see the instruments.

They drove for a long time. No one spoke. Now and then he saw trees or part of a cliff. Otherwise he saw nothing but snow.

The silence inside the car made him more and more nervous. Not just his family's silence—the car's silence, too. He couldn't even hear the car's tires on the road. He could hear the engine thrumming away but no sound of rubber against rock, dirt, or even packed snow. They might as well have been sailing through midair, for all he knew.

For a while he just stroked the dog on his lap. Then, feeling worried in a way he'd never felt before, Jake pushed Flash aside, eased away from the bundles on his right and left, and crawled over the passenger seat's back onto the seat beside Danielle. Jake sat down and carefully fastened the lap and shoulder belts. When Flash tried to follow him over, Jake pushed him back. *"Stay,"* he ordered.

Flash lingered a moment with his paws resting on

the back of Jake and Danielle's seat. Then he obeyed, settling into the spot Jake had just abandoned.

They drove and drove. Jake saw nothing but the car's headlights trying to shove their way through the storm.

Where are we? Jake wondered. Are we anywhere at all?

Suddenly Jake felt a big jolt. For a moment he seemed to be floating, weightless, just as he'd floated last spring, on the flight from the East Coast to Colorado, when the plane hit an air pocket and sank for what seemed like forever. Books, pillows, magazines, purses, even dinner trays and food had gone flying. The passengers had screamed and screamed till the plane stabilized.

This time no one screamed. There wasn't a chance.

THREE

▲

THE WHOLE THING STARTED, happened, and ended by the time Danielle realized what was going on. She felt her body yanked straight ahead as if by a huge invisible hand. The lap belt and chest restraint caught Danielle's torso like another hand, but her legs kicked upward against the seat in front of her and both arms flung forward, bashing into the seat back. Her head twisted downward, too, so that her chin jabbed hard into her chest. For a fraction of a second Danielle thought the two invisible hands might rip her in half. Then she felt herself flung backward again into the seat, and it was all over.

Everything was dead quiet for an instant.

She was too stunned to scream. Then all at once she felt so afraid that she started to cry.

Danielle heard the others just then: first Dad calling out with a strange stuttering sound, then Jake hollering right next to her, then Mom screaming so loud that the scream made Danielle's ears ring. The jumble of noises scared her even worse, but it also stopped her own wail. Shaking hard, aching all over, Danielle sat there in the dark and felt so frightened she couldn't cry anymore.

Then she reached up and switched on the car's overhead light.

What she saw turned out to be far worse than what she'd expected. Doubled over right next to her, Jake clutched the back of his neck and groaned. Mom was trying to claw her way closer to Dad. And Dad sat in the driver's seat trembling, coughing, and gasping like someone who had just dragged himself to shore after having nearly drowned.

Nothing made sense. Danielle couldn't believe this was happening. It seemed like a nightmare, the worst nightmare she'd ever had, but it went on and on and on.

It took a long time for everyone to calm down, still longer to figure out if anyone had been badly hurt.

Danielle and Jake seemed to be all right. Both of them felt achy, but neither had broken any bones.

Flash, too, was unharmed. He jumped frantically from the cargo area to the backseat, then back again, over and over, and sometimes he stopped to lick Jake and Danielle or to shove his nose against them. Danielle pushed the dog away but realized with a surge of delight that at least one member of the family seemed entirely unhurt.

The situation with Mom and Dad was something else altogether.

Mom had slammed her legs against the underside of the dashboard, hurting her knees. She kept saying, "It's okay, it's okay," but Danielle knew better. Tears came to Mom's eyes every time she moved. Even the heavy cloth of her slacks couldn't hide the swelling that grew worse and worse with each passing minute.

But Dad seemed far more seriously injured than anyone else. He looked okay—no cuts or bruises—yet something was clearly wrong. Even the slightest move caused him great pain. He couldn't even catch his breath without tensing up and squeezing his eyes shut. He kept his arms crossed over his chest as if to protect himself from an attack he expected at any moment.

"What is it?" Danielle asked him, forcing her head and shoulders through the space between the two front seats. "What's the matter?"

"Nothing!" he said through clenched teeth. "I'm—just—fine!"

"Is it your heart?" She felt terrified he might be having a heart attack.

"No! I'm—*fine!*"

"Dad, tell me. You have to tell me."

He shot her a sideways glance.

"You can't pretend nothing's wrong," she said.

Dad forced a smile.

Danielle felt furious at him when she saw that smile. He'd pretended from the start that nothing was wrong; that's what had gotten them in this whole mess to begin with. "It's not fair to *us*," she told him. "At least if we know what's wrong we can *do* something."

To her amazement, Danielle saw Dad's eyes well up with tears. He didn't cry, but seeing him get that close was something she'd never experienced before.

"Tell me what's wrong," Danielle said.

"Ribs."

"Broken ribs?"

Dad shook his head. "Nah—just—just banged 'em up a—" He clenched his teeth as he spoke the final word: "*bit.*" Even the effort of talking left his whole face pinched tight as a fist.

For a while—Danielle wasn't sure how long—everyone just sat there. No one moved much. No one even talked. Maybe they were too scared to talk. Maybe they were all trying to figure out what would happen next. She didn't like the silence but somehow understood that everyone needed it.

Danielle looked out the window on her left. She

saw nothing there but dim light and, accumulating on the outer edge of the car door, a rim of snow. Then her vision shifted and the glass became a mirror. She saw her own face there: dark brown hair, well-tanned skin, and fearful eyes staring back at her. The fear in those eyes made her look away, but not till Danielle had seen her brother's reflection in the window, too.

She turned to Jake. "You okay?" Danielle asked him.

He shrugged. She was used to seeing him shrug a lot—Jake thought shrugging made him look cool—but Danielle could tell he was worried.

"You sure?" she asked.

"I guess so," he said without meeting her gaze.

"You don't *look* so sure."

"I'm okay. Sore, that's all."

"Fine. Just checking."

Jake didn't say anything for a while. Both he and Danielle listened as Mom and Dad spoke in low voices up front.

"—as soon as—possible—"

"—question is how—"

"All right, all right—"

"—so what are you suggesting?"

They went on like this for a long time. Danielle couldn't hear them clearly but didn't need to. She knew that they were trying to figure out what to do next. It troubled her that they couldn't seem to agree. Then again, that didn't surprise her. How could they know? They were all in the middle of nowhere, in the dark, in a blizzard.

How could anyone know what to do?

FOUR

▲

Jake was amazed by how quickly the car cooled off. Within a few minutes after the accident he'd started feeling chilly; not long after that he could see his breath in the air when he exhaled. Then he remembered the cold-weather gear his parents had brought along. Parkas, wool caps, ski gloves, hiking boots . . . Jake rummaged around in the box and pulled out his coat. Putting it on warmed him up right away. Then he pulled out the other coats and passed them forward. Mom and Danielle put on theirs, too. Dad tried to put his on but somehow couldn't do it—Jake could hear him grinding his teeth from the pain of his effort—but eventually Danielle and Mom managed to help him out. Bundled up now, everyone felt somewhat better. Yet soon enough the car's interior got so cold that Jake started shivering.

He checked his watch. A quarter to six. He wondered what it might feel like to spend the night there.

Time after time Dad tried starting the engine. Jake heard a lot of grinding sounds that never quite got the car going again. Now and then Mom would say, "You're draining the battery," and Dad would tell her, "Just one more time," and he'd try again, but the car still wouldn't start. Then suddenly the grinding noises went faster and faster till the engine roared to life.

Everyone cheered.

"Yes!" Jake shouted.

Dad laughed and immediately doubled over in pain.

When he recovered, though, he switched on the wipers. The blades struggled a moment, then shoved what must have been two inches of snow off the windshield. Almost at once Jake saw the glass turning white. Beyond the whiteness he couldn't see much of anything but deep gray.

Dad turned on the headlights.

"*No!*" Mom groaned, as if her refusal to acknowledge what she saw would make it disappear.

The car's right front fender and its hood had crumpled up to make a peak from what had previously been flat metal. Two rough-barked pine trees slanted side by side as if growing out of the fender itself. Yet even as they stared, this sight grew dim in the snowfall.

* * *

After that, things got even worse. When Dad tried backing the car out, the rear tires whined and skidded but the car itself didn't even budge. Jake and Danielle then stepped out briefly to see what might be the matter. Just a few minutes outside made it clear how much was wrong. The Darcys' car had struck the trees hard enough to crunch the fender against the right front tire; the bent fender now gripped the tire like a wrench. Even if they could have pried the fender loose, however, the car had gone off the road and come to rest pointing downward on a fairly steep slope. Worst of all, the car had bogged down in about ten inches of powdery snow. Even a tow truck would have had a hard time pulling the Darcys' car out.

"So what are we going to do?" Mom asked.

"I don't—know," Dad replied, struggling to get the words out. "I just—don't—know."

Jake felt frightened by the sound of fear in his parents' voices. He folded his arms across his chest and hunched over against the cold, though he knew it wasn't just the cold he wanted to keep out. He wanted to be somewhere else. He wanted something else to be happening. He wanted this accident to be over and everyone to be okay. For a moment he started to cry. Then, worried that someone might notice, he nuzzled against Flash to hide his face.

"Maybe we can flag down a passing car," Mom said.

"A passing car?" Jake huffed. "Who else but us would be dumb enough to be driving around up here?"

Dad turned toward Jake; then at once he twisted back, as if someone had suddenly jabbed him in the chest. Quietly he said, "I didn't—get in an—accident on—purpose."

Jake wanted to apologize but wasn't sure what to say.

Mom went on: "Maybe someone with a cabin up here—"

"Jeannine," Dad said, breathing hard, "it's a—min-ing—road."

"And even if someone drove by," Jake added, "that might not happen for hours."

"You have any better ideas?" Mom asked.

"Maybe—" Danielle spoke just that one word, then stopped short. "Maybe Jake and I should hike down to the interstate."

"The *interstate*," Mom said, sounding as if Danielle had suggested walking to the moon.

"Mom, we can't just sit here waiting for someone to come by and rescue us."

"Do you have any idea how far we've come up this road?"

Dad glanced at the dashboard. "I don't know—I

should have—checked the—the—odometer. But I—didn't. Five miles? Six or—seven?"

"Boy, have I got news for you!" Jake exclaimed.

Everyone turned to stare at him.

He couldn't wait to set them straight. He wasn't sure why he'd noted the dashboard instruments on the way up. Maybe it was simply to reassure himself when he was feeling nervous. In any case, he'd done it. "I checked the odometer just as we pulled off the highway. You know how far it is to the interstate? Twenty-point-eight miles!"

"All right, twenty-point-eight miles," Danielle said wearily.

"You know how long it would take to walk that far?"

"Don't be such a nerd," Danielle muttered.

"Walking at a speed of two miles per hour—"

Suddenly Danielle shouted, "Stop it! This isn't math class! This isn't a math problem!"

"Let me explain—"

"Don't bother. We get the point."

Jake, feeling hurt, glared at his sister.

Mom said, "I want both of you to calm down. I don't care how far it is. You simply are not leaving this car."

"Mom—"

"You are not going for help."

"But Mom—"

"I—totally—agree," Dad blurted, shoving the words out. "Neither of you—is going—*anywhere*."

Jake interrupted before Dad could continue: "So what are we supposed to do, sit here till we freeze to death?"

Mom turned to stare at him. Jake couldn't make sense of the expression on his mother's face. Mom didn't look angry so much as disgusted. "How can you talk like that?" she asked. "No one's going to die. We're all going to be fine. Just be patient. Everything's going to work out just fine." She laughed suddenly.

Jake said, "Yeah? How's that?"

"Dad or I will go for help," Mom replied.

"Get real, Mom."

Dad twisted around. "Jake, don't—talk like—" Then his pain got the best of him, and he slumped back in his seat.

At this point Danielle said, "Jake's right. It's not realistic to think either of you could go."

"No—we will," Mom said. "*I* will."

"But how?"

"Somehow. I don't know—"

"Mom, you can't even *stand*," Danielle said. "How can you walk all the way down—"

"I'll go," Dad interrupted, doing his best to speak without faltering.

"Dad—"

"I'll be—fine."

"Dad, it doesn't make sense."

He didn't answer. Instead, he began zipping up his coat and putting on his gloves. Jake couldn't see him well from where he sat, but he could hear Dad's breathing grow louder and more frantic as he tried getting ready. Dad started grunting, too, until the grunts became a constant moan.

What Jake heard terrified him. Dad would die out there. He'd have a coronary. He'd stumble off a cliff.

Yet even as Mom and Danielle started shouting, Dad unlocked the door and pushed it open. A blast of snowy air rushed in at once. Jake twisted away, his face stinging, eyes squinting, hair blowing about. He turned back in time to see Dad swing around and, with a muffled cry, force himself out of the car. At once the door slammed shut.

Flash barked furiously, but no one spoke. Jake, Danielle, and Mom glanced at each other, all of them looking too bewildered to move. Jake turned to stare out the window. He could see Dad out there a few yards away. Then suddenly he was gone.

"Something happened," Jake said.

"Where is he?" Mom asked.

Jake shoved his way past Danielle to peer out the window. "He's—I can't see him," Jake said frantically.

Then Mom, her voice sounding desperate, stammered, *"Go help your father!"*

FIVE

▲

DANIELLE WAS THE FIRST ONE out. She didn't even take time to zip her coat or pull on her ski cap. She just shoved open the door and bounded out.

The wind grabbed her in an icy embrace, nearly ripped her coat off, and left her gasping. The air was thick with snow. Even the snow on the ground seemed in motion, welling up to her knees like water in a fast-moving stream as she waded through it. Powder, the Colorado skiers called it. Not like wet Eastern snow—nothing you could dig your boots into. More like dust: billowing even as it fell, blinding her as she tried to find her way. She couldn't believe how hard the wind struck her. She'd experienced some rough weather at Mountain Mastery, but nothing like this.

"Dad!" she yelled. Danielle stopped, stood still, and listened for an answer.

All she heard was the wind's shriek.

No matter where she looked—backward, forward, off to the sides—Danielle couldn't see her dad. Worse yet, she couldn't even see the car. Then the wind gusted again and she couldn't see anything at all. Only snow.

Just then something jolted into Danielle so hard that she lost her balance and fell facedown in the snow. She flailed about, sputtering and choking, till she managed to roll onto her left side.

At some point she realized that a hand was helping her up: tugging at her right arm.

"Danielle—"

She swung about to see Jake standing beside her. She felt so furious that she forced herself up, then frantically brushed herself off. "What are you *doing!*" she shouted at her brother.

"What do you *think* I'm doing?"

She ignored him. "Where's Dad?" Danielle felt more and more desperate as she looked around, trying to see past the snowfall. "I don't even know where the car is."

"It's all right."

"What d'you mean, all right?"

"Danielle—"

She started shouting again: "Dad! Dad!"

"Danielle, *look.*"

Danielle saw what her brother had been trying to

show her. He held a coil of rope from the gear Dad kept in the Blazer. The rope itself ran out of his hands and disappeared into the storm. "What's this?" she asked angrily.

"Dad's towrope!" Jake shouted over the wind. "I tied one end to a door handle! We can use it like a tether, then follow it back if we get lost!"

She understood at once. Danielle felt a flicker of hope.

"Ready?"

"Ready!"

They scrambled up the slope. Snow churned around their legs. What scared her most of all was how little she could see. Everything was white. No matter where she looked, Danielle saw nothing but snow.

"Dad!" she shouted.

Jake shouted, too.

Using the tether as their guide, they walked to the right a while, played out a few yards of rope, then walked to the left, played out more rope, then headed right again. They figured that this zigzag pattern gave them the best chance of finding Dad. Yet after five or ten minutes they not only hadn't found him, they weren't even sure if they'd spotted his tracks. The wind swept their own path clean, too.

Suddenly both Danielle and Jake stumbled over something. Jake took a step, then lost his balance and fell to one side. At once he forced himself up and started tugging at a big mass in the snow. Danielle saw with amazement that it was their father. Crouched on all fours, he was almost entirely white. She rushed closer and helped Jake try to pull him up.

"Dad—Dad, are you all right?"

He just moaned. His eyes were squeezed tight, and he shook harder than she'd ever seen anyone shake before.

All she could understand him say was "—for help—"

Jake shouted, "We'll get you back to the car!"

"Help him up!" Danielle yelled at her brother.

For a long time they struggled to help Dad stand. Danielle started to wonder if they'd ever succeed. Maybe Dad was already half frozen. Maybe he'd flounder and collapse in the snow. Maybe he'd be the first of them to die, and the rest would soon follow.

Somehow they managed. They got him upright and led him back, following their lifeline to the car.

SIX

▲

gotten Dad into the Blazer, Jake crawled over the rear
seat and curled up with Flash in the cargo area.
Holding the dog felt good. Flash was warm—wonder-
fully warm after Jake had gotten so cold out there in
the snow. Flash was calm, too. He tended to be calm
anyway, but to Jake he seemed even calmer than
usual at a time when everyone else in the family was
hassling one another about the fix they were in.

"—could have got yourself killed—"

"—didn't exactly *plan* it that way—"

"—and give Dad a chance—"

Jake listened to Mom, Dad, and Danielle hash over
this latest close call. He and Danielle had barely
made it back to the car. Dad had struggled hard simply to stay on his feet. Danielle and Jake had almost
lost their grip on him and let him fall again. Only the

tether had prevented them from heading off in the wrong direction.

Jake felt proud of that tether. Using it had been just a hunch—he'd seen a movie recently that showed weightless astronauts connected by tethers to the space shuttle *Discovery*—but the idea had worked. The tether had made it possible to find Dad in the first place; then it let them all work their way back. He felt pleased that a good idea could make so much difference. Not that this was the first time: Jake had always prided himself on his ability to improvise. He'd even entered contests in which the participants had to solve a problem or invent something with limited materials in just a short while. Yet regardless of what he'd done with the tether, Jake felt worried anyway. It would take a lot more than a towrope to get his family back to Denver alive.

Flash nuzzled against his cheek while Jake petted him and scratched behind his ears. The dog seemed unusually quiet. He almost seemed to know what big trouble they were in.

"Got any brainstorms?" Jake asked Flash. "Want to go down through the snow like a Saint Bernard and bring back help?"

Flash turned away and rested his snout on Jake's thigh.

"I don't blame you," Jake said.

What they really needed, Jake thought to himself, was another good idea. Not an idea that *seemed* good, like slogging almost twenty-one miles down a snowy road to the interstate. What they needed was an idea that cut through their problems quick and clean as a laser. Something clever. Something simple. Something quick. But of course to have a good idea they needed to know what they were facing. In this case, that meant the weather. And they couldn't know about the weather without a weather report—

Jake sat forward so abruptly that Flash panicked and jumped off his lap. At once Jake turned to his sister.

"Danielle."

"What." Danielle barely glanced his way. Some of her dark hair, now wet from the storm, hung down her face in limp tendrils.

"I need to talk with you."

"All right, so talk."

"In private."

Danielle swung about in her seat. "Private?" she asked. "So what should we do, reserve a conference room?"

"Give me a break." Jake could have shut her out but decided not to. This was too important. If he could just convince Danielle that his new idea made sense . . .

"Let's step outside a moment."

"Outside? You're crazy!" Danielle exclaimed. "I've barely warmed up from last time."

"Danielle—" He didn't say more. Somehow he didn't need to. His sister must have picked up on something—his tone of voice or expression—and she seemed willing to believe him.

"Okay," she said.

Jake expected his parents to protest, but they didn't. Maybe they didn't even hear their discussion. Dad was too uncomfortable; Mom was too busy trying to help Dad settle in.

Danielle and Jake pulled on their hiking boots again, zipped up their coats, and slipped outside before their parents could stop them.

SEVEN

▲

"WE CAN'T HIKE DOWN TO THE interstate," Jake told Danielle as they huddled together beside the Blazer. "I figure that would take at least twelve hours."

"I hear you," Danielle said wearily. She couldn't believe that Jake had coaxed her out of the car just to say something so obvious.

"Maybe fourteen, fifteen hours in snow like this."

"Jake, what's the alternative?"

Jake seemed to be waiting for just those words. Pulling out the Colorado map, he told her, "Look." He pointed to a little triangle south of Millertown. The wind kept yanking at the map, and snow hissed across its surface. "That's Mount Remington."

"So?" Danielle couldn't see why it mattered.

"We're just west of it."

"What difference does it make—"

"We can climb the mountain," Jake announced proudly.

Danielle was so furious she almost couldn't speak. "Mom and Dad are both hurt really bad—"

"Danielle, listen—"

"—and you want to go *mountain climbing?*"

"Danielle, there's a weather station up there. At the top."

"A weather station!" She couldn't believe anyone could be so dumb.

"I heard about it on a TV news program," Jake told her, then rattled on about how, at an altitude of more than fourteen thousand feet, it was the highest weather station in the continental United States.

"Great," Danielle countered. "Just what we need—a weather station."

Jake wouldn't give up. "Danielle, there's a team of meteorologists up there. All year round. And they've got radio contact with the outside world."

Now she started to see why her brother was pressing the point so hard. The guys at the weather station could radio for assistance. A search and rescue team could reach Mom and Dad quicker than if Jake and Danielle slogged all the way down to the highway. Yet Danielle wasn't convinced that Jake's idea would help them now. "That's just wonderful," she said. "But what's the point if the meteorologists are up there and we're down here?"

"Plenty—provided we let them know what's happened. And we can probably get up there a lot quicker than we'd get to the interstate."

"Jake, that mountain's fourteen thousand feet tall."

"Right. And we're already at ten or eleven thousand, easily."

"But that still means three or four thousand to go."

"I know that—I'm not stupid. But it's still a far shorter distance for us than going all the way down to the interstate. I estimate we'd need maybe five hours to reach the summit."

Danielle was silent for a while, just thinking. Meteorologists . . . Five hours . . . To let them know what's happened . . . She said, "Right," then fell silent again. "But Jake—how would we get there?"

"You tell me," Jake said. "That's your department."

Now she understood what he was saying. Just that summer, Danielle had spent two weeks at a Mountain Mastery camp in the Colorado Rockies learning basic mountaineering technique and wilderness survival skills. Those weeks had been one of the hardest times in her whole life but one of the best times, too. She had climbed cliffs, dangled from ropes, and walked all day with a heavy pack on her back. Even the ordinary events had been a challenge: bathing in an icy mountain stream, sleeping on the ground without a tent, eating gritty plants she'd found in the forest. Every day Danielle wondered if she could tolerate the challenges ahead. Yet somehow she'd done just that. The Mountain Mastery course had been an ordeal, yet she completed it successfully and left feeling different—stronger, braver, and more sure of herself.

And so Danielle felt both intrigued and alarmed by Jake's idea. On the one hand, climbing Mount Remington wasn't out of the question. She had learned enough about climbing technique to have climbed three big peaks with her teammates and instructors. Danielle didn't know anything about Mount Remington, but she knew from what she'd heard during the summer that Colorado's Front Range peaks—the mountains along the eastern edge of the Rockies—generally weren't as challenging as others in the state. On the other hand, she thought her brother's idea was totally outrageous. They didn't have the right supplies. They didn't have the right climbing gear. They didn't have the right knowledge to pull off such a crazy stunt.

Jake's idea would get them both killed—and doom their parents, too.

EIGHT

▲

JAKE DIDN'T INTEND TO TELL his parents what he'd suggested to Danielle. He knew they'd reject the plan right off. Besides, Jake wasn't even sure if it would really work. Maybe Danielle was right. Maybe climbing the mountain would be too difficult. Yet he wasn't convinced that slogging down to the interstate would work, either. Jake didn't know what to do. All he knew was that convincing his parents even to let him and Danielle hike out would be hard enough.

"Absolutely not," Dad said when Danielle finished explaining how they'd backtrack to the highway.

"This isn't such a great idea," Mom said.

"We never said it was a great idea," Danielle replied. "Just the only one we've got."

Mom shook her head. "It's far too risky."

Jake took a turn at trying to persuade them. "So

what isn't risky?" he asked. "Hiking out will be risky, but so is sitting here. I've been keeping track of the temperature." Jake held out the little zipper-pull thermometer he wore on his parka. "When we were outside last, the temp had dropped to twenty-three degrees. It's not even nine o'clock yet. What if it keeps getting colder and colder?"

"All the more reason to sit tight and stay warm," Mom said.

"We—can run the—car," Dad said between desperate breaths.

"Right," Danielle said, "assuming the engine keeps working."

"And assuming the gas holds out," Jake added.

No one spoke for a while. Jake could see both Mom and Dad staring at the gas gauge. It showed less than half a tank.

Before Jake could continue, Danielle got the jump on him. "Here's how I see it," she said. "Mom's right—it's risky to hike out. Too risky to do at night, anyway. We should probably stay put till morning. After that, it's anyone's guess. At Mountain Mastery they told me it gets real cold after Colorado snowstorms. The snow lets up, the sky clears, and the temperature drops through the floor. If someone finds us soon, we'll probably be all right. But if we sit here and no one comes, then we're really stuck. We'll probably end up hypothermic—"

"That's when your body temperature drops so low," said Jake, "that it throws your whole system out of whack. Your heart can't function right. Your hypothalamus—"

"All right, we get the picture," Danielle told him.

"I'm just explaining."

"We don't need a lecture."

"Just go on," Mom said.

"All I'm telling you," said Danielle, "is that I think it's a bigger risk for everyone to stay put than for some of us to go for help."

"We just—can't let—let you face the—elements," Dad said.

Danielle forced a laugh. "Elements? Jake and I will probably be warmer on the move than you and Mom will be just sitting here."

Dad didn't respond, so Jake thought maybe his sister had won the point.

"I still don't think this is a good idea," Mom said once again.

"I don't either," Dad said.

Jake looked at his watch. Nine o'clock. Before anyone else could speak he said, "Let's wait till morning. Then we'll decide. We can't do much till then anyway."

NINE

▲

THAT WAS THE WORST NIGHT OF
Danielle's entire life. She was cold, hungry, sore, and
exhausted, yet physical discomforts were the least of
what bothered her.

Danielle and her family had a few supplies to get
them through the night. Mom and Jake had packed
enough food to allow everyone a good-sized snack of
one sandwich apiece, a big bag of potato chips to
divvy up, some granola bars, and one serving each
of hot cocoa from a thermos. There was a share of
food for every member of the family to have the next
day, too: a few more granola bars and another small
serving of cocoa. Flash had his own food supply,
since Mom had packed a bag of the beagle's dry dog
chow. And Danielle knew they stood a chance
against the cold because the Darcys had brought
along some quilts among the winter things intended

for the mountain house. They even had a first aid kit with some aspirin to help ease everyone's aches. They weren't about to starve or to die of their injuries.

No, what made the night miserable wasn't so easily soothed as a painful knee or a growling stomach. It was something beyond what Danielle's family could do to help her.

Mostly she was just scared. Scared to be stuck in the mountains. Scared to be hiding in a messed-up car. Scared to be trapped in a blizzard. Scared to be right there with her parents—both of them badly hurt—yet unable to help them. Danielle had never thought she could feel so scared.

No one slept much that night. They tried, they pretended, but they failed. There wasn't enough room. Mom and Dad needed as much space as possible to ease the pressure on their injuries, so they scooted the front seats backward. That didn't really help much—Mom couldn't stretch out enough to relieve her throbbing legs—but it certainly succeeded in cramping Danielle and Jake. Danielle tried curling up on the passenger seat but without much luck: she kept bumping into her brother. Then for a while Jake climbed into the cargo area with Flash. That gave Danielle more room, but not for long. The cargo area was full of Dad's gear—ropes, toolboxes, field equipment—and Jake couldn't get comfortable. Besides, it was so much colder back there that he couldn't stay warm. After twenty minutes or so he moved back beside his sister.

Even when Danielle managed to doze off, it wasn't for long. Jake's snoring was the least of her problems, though he made more noise while asleep than anyone their age Danielle had ever been around. The car's noises weren't the worst of it, either, though the entire vehicle clicked and thumped during the twenty-minute intervals when Dad shut the engine off, and though it rattled and rumbled during the alternate intervals when he ran the engine. Danielle could have tolerated all that racket easily enough. Instead, what really troubled her was hearing Dad and Mom moan during the few times when they fell asleep. It wasn't that Danielle resented the noise they made; rather, she felt more and more frightened by the sound. She wanted to help them but didn't know what to do. Danielle didn't know what she *could* do. They seemed so helpless, so vulnerable, as if Danielle and Jake were the parents now and Mom and Dad were the children. . . .

"Hey!"

Danielle shoved herself up from the car seat. She saw Jake's dim shape leaning close to her. She whispered, "What!"

"Are you okay?"

"I guess so." After a second she asked, "Are you?"

"Yeah, wonderful."

For a while they simply sat there in the dark.

Then Danielle heard Jake whisper again:

"You really think we can hike out of here?"

"We have to."

"But you think we can get down there in time—"

"Shh!" Danielle heard Mom stirring up ahead. After a pause Danielle said, "Later."

"But don't you think by the time we'd get down there—"

"*Later.* Go to sleep."

"So who's sleeping?"

"Not me, that's for sure," Danielle said. "At least not with you bugging me."

Somehow she dozed off. Right away Danielle started to dream.

It's summer. Danielle is with her friends at Mountain Mastery. There are ten or twelve others with her, all of them in their midteens except for the two instructors, and they are deep in the wilderness. They're working their way up a mountainside. Heaps of stone rubble slope downward to the right; a cliff angles sharply upward to the left. Danielle watches her own feet find their places step by step on the trail ahead. In this dangerous place, even the smallest stumble could be fatal. The pack rides heavily on her back.

She has never worked harder in her life, yet she can't remember being happier. The air is cool and dry. The sky is cloudless, altogether blue, perfect. A breeze rises from the valley carrying the scent of pine trees and wildflowers. Danielle is panting from the effort of the hike, yet she feels good, strong, fit, ready to tackle any obstacle ahead. Best of all, she's with her friends—the girls and guys in Danielle's Mountain Mastery group, a group she's learned to trust literally with her life.

Now they're not on a slope; they're halfway up a cliff. Having practiced for days, everyone knows what to do. Handholds. Footholds. Ropecraft. Belay techniques. Everything the instructors have taught them. Yet it's different now—this is a real mountain. Danielle isn't entirely sure she can live up to everyone's expectations. Or even her own.

It's Danielle's turn to climb. Sam, a sixteen year old who Danielle thinks really likes her, is right above her on the cliff. He's taking in the belay rope as Danielle works her way from one move to the next. Alison, one of the instructors, is coaching both Sam and Danielle from where she sits next to Sam. The footholds and handholds seem more and more difficult to find. Clinging to the cliff by her toes and fingertips, Danielle gradually sees that she might actually fall.

"Give her some slack," Alison tells Sam. "She's doing fine."

"I am *not*," Danielle wants to shout, but she can't spare the breath. She's gasping now—working so hard she can't get enough air. Danielle has broken into a cold sweat. At some point she starts wondering if her hands will get so slippery that she'll just slide right off the mountain.

Now Alison's voice comes down the cliff to Danielle: "Quit struggling! You're too tense! You're going to shake yourself loose!"

It's not the risk of falling that terrifies Danielle. She knows the belay rope will catch her. But to fall in front of everyone—that's what she fears.

At precisely that instant, Danielle's boots lose their grip on the granite supporting them. Her legs and torso drop, yanking her hands from where they so desperately grope at the cliff. She can feel herself plummeting fast. The rope will catch her at any moment.

But it doesn't. Danielle feels a small tug—nothing more. No jolt around the waist. No impact of her body pulled short and shoved into the cliff. Just the tickle of the air rushing past her.

She glances up to see Sam, Alison, and all the rest fading from view as she falls. The cliff tumbles out of view. The sky whirls by, the valley rushes past, the sky shoots past again: valley, sky, valley, sky, over and over.

And she's falling, falling, falling not just from the mountain to the rocks below but from warmth into cold, from summer into autumn, from midday light on a mountainside into darkness in a snowbound Blazer where Danielle wakes abruptly, forcing herself upright, gasping for breath.

TEN

▲

"WHAT ARE YOU DOING BACK there, anyway? Jake—answer me."

Jake heard Mom's voice from where he crouched in the Blazer's cargo area, but he didn't respond. He was too busy rummaging around.

"Jake, what on earth are you doing?"

"Nothing."

"Then stop making so much racket."

He tried to move more carefully. The fact was, he couldn't see well in the dawn's half-light. Most of what he knew about the stuff back there he had to determine by touch alone. The toolbox was especially frustrating—so many things inside, many of the tools similar to one another, all of them packed into a small space. Still, it seemed important to do what he could.

Jake hefted his pack. He couldn't believe how heavy it was. Fifteen pounds at least, maybe eighteen or twenty. For a moment he felt a temptation to dump everything out. He'd gotten carried away. This was all a lot of nonsense. Worse than nonsense: craziness. He and Danielle would succeed in finding help only if they moved fast, and moving fast meant traveling light. Dragging all this stuff around definitely wasn't traveling light.

And yet . . . And yet . . . They couldn't do what needed to be done, he told himself, if they didn't have the means to do it. And Jake wasn't really sure what they needed, so he had to take a chance. He had to give himself some options.

Now he heard Danielle's voice: "Jake."

"What."

"Whatever you're doing, knock it off."

"I'm not hurting anyone."

"You're making so much noise it's bothering Mom and Dad."

In the pause that followed, Jake could hear his dad's labored breathing. Was Dad awake or asleep? Could anyone sleep while working that hard simply to breathe?

Jake understood just then what was about to happen. This wasn't going to be one of those competitions where he matched his wits against the clock and tried to invent something. This wasn't going to be the Wing It Fling It Contest or the Better Mousetrap Derby. This was going to be—well, the real thing. This was going to be an event where everything he and Danielle did really mattered. Mattered more than anything either of them had ever done.

Then Danielle's voice again: "As soon as they're awake, let's get going."

Everyone tried to pretend it was no big deal. Mom and Dad acted so calm that Jake and Danielle might simply have been heading off to a ball game or a weekend visit with relatives.

"You think you'll be warm enough?" Mom asked.

"We'll be fine," Danielle answered.

"Make sure—you've got your—ski cap," Dad said. "It's pure—wool."

"I've already got it," Jake assured him.

"Don't forget your lunch," Mom said as she held out a paper bag and the thermos.

Jake knew what was in there: granola bars in the bag, hot chocolate in the thermos, all of it food that Mom and Dad should have eaten for breakfast but had saved for Jake and Danielle's trip instead. "Why don't you keep it?" Jake asked, pushing the bag away.

"You two will—need it more than—we do," Dad managed to say.

Danielle objected: "No, *you* will."

"Take it."

"Dad."

"You'll need the—energy."

Reluctantly, Jake took the supplies from Mom. He started to open his backpack, then hesitated. He didn't want to reveal how much stuff he'd crammed in there already. Hoping Danielle would take the hint, Jake held out the lunch bag and thermos. She faltered a moment. Did she resent the burden, he wondered? If only she knew how much *he* was carrying! Yet Jake couldn't tell her; that would ruin everything. Luckily, Danielle opened up her own pack without further complaint and put in both the thermos and the bag.

Then Dad gave them some extra money, just as he always did when Jake and Danielle left for a trip, as if they might stop somewhere down the road for burgers and fries. He even made a joke when he handed over the cash: "Don't spend it—all in one—place."

But soon there was nothing more to say. Danielle and Jake glanced at each other. Danielle said, "Well, I guess we'd better go."

Dad said, "I guess you'd—better."

"Stay warm," Jake said.

"Of course," Mom said, smiling.

"We'll be back in no time."

"Of course you will."

"Don't—worry about—us," Dad said. "We'll—be toasty—warm."

Silence lingered like the vapor they all exhaled into the cold air.

Danielle slipped on her backpack and took hold of the door handle.

Before she could open the door, though, Dad forced himself around in his seat and said, "I'm sorry—sorry I got us all—in this—this—*mess.*"

Jake could see the tears in Dad's eyes. Maybe they were partly from the pain of turning, Jake told himself, but he knew that wasn't the only reason. Jake reached out and set his hand on Dad's right shoulder. Dad flinched hard. Jake pulled his hand back, not wanting to hurt him, but at once Dad reached across his chest with his left hand and held it out till Jake reached back again. Jake squeezed Dad's hand. Then Danielle did the same. Then they both reached out to Mom as well as possible past the seats and headrests.

"Bye," Danielle said.

"See you soon," Jake said.

"Bye," Dad told them.

"Please be careful," Mom said.

Before anyone could get upset, Danielle pulled open the door and climbed out.

Jake grabbed his pack and followed her at once.

ELEVEN

▲

THE STORM HAD EASED. Danielle noticed the difference right away as she and Jake left the car. Snow kept falling, though not nearly as hard as during the night before. By now the snow actually fell instead of blowing sideways. The snowfall looked much thinner, too—thin enough that Danielle could see the snowdrifts around her, the trees rising beyond the drifts, and even some of the land looming beyond the trees. The clouds overhead must have been thinning as well, for the sky didn't look so gloomy now. Just the thought of the blizzard letting up boosted Danielle's spirits. Soon they'd be out of there. The whole ordeal would be over. Everything would be all right.

"Ready?" Jake asked as they wallowed off.

At just that moment, however, a sharp pang of

loneliness hit Danielle. She wanted to tell Mom and Dad good-bye again. She glanced back at the car. The front end was sunken deep in snow, and snow had drifted over the far side halfway up the roof. Danielle found it hard to believe that Mom and Dad were stuck inside, both of them badly hurt, with little more than a few quilts, a small dog, and the car's idling motor to keep them from freezing to death. The loneliness she felt now turned suddenly to fear. If she and Jake didn't get down to the interstate . . .

A second good-bye would just make things worse, she decided. This was hard enough already. Danielle turned just then, headed off, and scrambled up the snowy slope to the road.

Or what she thought was the road. She couldn't actually see it. What she saw was a winding trench formed by the trees on each side, a trench whose bottom was filled with snow. And as she and Jake struggled down this trench, Danielle realized at once how much more difficult their task would be than she'd first thought.

The snow was about a foot deep even in the shallowest places. Where the snow had drifted, it was two or three feet deep, sometimes deeper. Danielle and Jake tried to find the easy way through: anywhere that seemed relatively level. Yet it never quite worked out right, and time after time both of them ended up in snowdrifts so deep that they floundered up to their thighs. Going just a few hundred feet took furious effort. In no time at all they were exhausted.

For the next half hour, Danielle and Jake staggered down the road. Sometimes the snow reached no higher than their knees, and they made good progress. Sometimes they plunged in far deeper—thigh-deep, even waist-deep—and hardly got anywhere at all. Panting, gasping, grunting, both of them spent more effort staying upright than going forward. Once or twice they even lost their footing and toppled over. Danielle gasped from the snow that got up her sleeves and down her collar. Soon she resented the effort that every step took. Traveling at this rate, she couldn't imagine how they'd ever make it down to I-70. They'd wear out long before that. They'd bog down. They'd wallow into a deep drift and sink out of sight.

"That was pretty clever what you did with the rope," Danielle said during one of their frequent rests.

Her brother shrugged. "There's lots of things you can learn without going to Mountain Mastery."

"I'm just thanking you, all right? I'm not trying to keep score."

"Fine."

She felt annoyed by his response and fell silent for a while. Then curiosity got the best of her. "How'd you think that up, anyway?"

Again he shrugged. "I just thought of it."

"Good for you." She set off again.

They hit a particularly bad patch soon afterward—a bend in the road where drifts had accumulated even deeper than what they'd found so far. Both Danielle and Jake had to take ridiculously big steps, raising their feet high and plunging them down again, to make any headway at all. Within a few minutes they were both winded. They stopped right beside each other and rested again.

"We don't have to be doing this," Jake said abruptly.

"Excuse me?" Danielle wasn't sure she'd heard right.

"I said we don't really have to do this."

She stood there a long time, panting, listening to her heart thump, and wondering how she could stay patient with him. What did he have in mind—maybe sprouting wings and *flying* down?

But before Danielle could speak, Jake started in again about the mountain climb. Mount Remington. The weather station at the top. The meteorologists living there. The communications gear those guys could use to call for help. Talking loudly, gesturing wildly, Jake went through the whole thing all over again.

"Look, it's a clever idea," Danielle said, interrupting him. "It's good you mentioned it. But it's too—" She wanted to say more but couldn't. The words vanished like the breath she exhaled into the cold air.

"Too what?" Jake asked, sounding grumpy.

Danielle had a whole argument figured out. She would explain her reservations. She would appeal to Jake's rational mind. She would avoid bruising his ego. Then, having set him straight, she would continue slogging down the road. Jake would follow without protest.

Instead, Danielle blurted, "It's totally nuts! How are we supposed to climb this mountain? *Us? Now?*"

"Same way we'd climb any mountain."

"But we don't have any climbing gear—no rope, no hardware, none of what we'd need. We don't even have any food. How do we climb a mountain without gear and food?"

Jake's only answer was a smile. Danielle saw the smile and knew at once what it meant. She wasn't at all surprised when Jake took off his pack, pulled it open, and showed her what was inside. The pack was full of stuff—so much stuff she couldn't even see it all.

"What's this?" she asked.

"Tools," he told her.

"What do you mean, *tools?*"

"Tools from Dad's toolbox. Other things, too. Things I thought might come in handy."

What she saw looked like ordinary hand tools. "A hammer?" Danielle wondered out loud. "A carpenter's hammer on a mountain climb?"

"There's a whole bunch of screwdrivers, too."

"Great—just what we need."

"But you said we needed tools."

"We do. *Climbing* tools," Danielle said, more and more impatient. She already knew enough about one of her brother's hobbies: improvising gadgets out of odds and ends. He'd even won a contest back in New Jersey. Allowed only a paper cup, two rubber bands, a ruler, and six thumbtacks, the contestants were supposed to invent a functioning mousetrap. Jake not only built one quicker than anyone else; his trap was also the only one that really worked. But this situation was different. This wasn't a game—it was a matter of life and death. "This stuff won't do," she told him.

"Well, it's all we've got," he responded. "We'll just have to make the best of it."

Danielle lost her temper. "Can't you understand? We need a rope. Jake—a rope! We can't climb the mountain without a rope."

Just then Jake pulled out something that Danielle recognized at once: Dad's towrope.

"Voilà!" he shouted.

"All right, it's a rope," Danielle admitted. "But it's not a *climbing* rope."

"Beggars can't be choosers, right?"

Feeling more and more uneasy, Danielle groped about for reasons not to proceed. "What about food? On a climb like that we won't get far without food."

Jake pulled out a small, lumpy brown paper bag and a thermos.

"Three granola bars and a few cups of cocoa?" Danielle asked in amazement. "How far will *that* get us?"

At these words, Jake tugged out something else from his pack: a plastic bag full of Flash's Critter Fritters.

"Dog food!" Danielle shouted. "No way!"

"It's better than nothing."

"Jake, I'm not eating dog food."

"All right—I'll eat your share, too."

"This is crazy," Danielle told him.

"Crazier than plodding along—"

"Jake—"

"How long has it been since we left the car?" he asked suddenly.

Danielle glanced at her watch. "Almost an hour."

"And how far do you figure we've come?"

"I don't know. Maybe half a mile."

"At that rate it'll take us thirty-five, maybe forty hours—"

"But how long will it take us to backtrack all the way to the car?"

"We don't have to backtrack anywhere. We'll just head east from here."

"How come you're so sure?"

"The peak is real long," Jake said, sounding totally confident. "I saw panoramic shots of it on TV. We can start climbing anywhere along its length."

Danielle couldn't shake her sense of unease. "Jake, we'll get killed climbing that peak."

"Maybe so," Jake admitted. "But if we don't at least try, we'll be dead anyway. And Mom and Dad will be, too."

"We can't climb Mount Remington."

"No? Then let's just give up."

"I didn't say anything about giving up."

"Maybe you should've. Going down the road *seems* to make sense, but it doesn't. Not really. Not in snow this deep. Not in snow halfway up to your waist."

"But on the mountain—"

"The wind up there will blow it clean. Believe me."

"Jake, it sounds so crazy," Danielle said in despair.

"Maybe so, but I think it'll work."

"Jake—*how?*"

"I don't really know. I just think it will. And you have to think so, too, or we're sunk. Danielle, it's climb or die."

TWELVE

▲

AND SO THEY LEFT THE ROAD, worked their way through the drifts piled up along the edge, and reached a kind of promontory that looked off to the east. Jake could tell they were facing east because the sky looked so bright there. He couldn't see the sun, but the glare shifting through the clouds told him it was somewhere beyond.

The mountain was, too. Across the valley, behind the clouds. Mount Remington.

"That's where we have to go," Jake said, gesturing outward. "Right across this low area. Then up."

He could tell that Danielle still wasn't convinced. She took in the view without saying a word.

"I guess we'd better get going," he told her.

Then, just as she seemed ready to come along, the storm shifted. The snowfall didn't stop; it simply thinned for a few moments. What had seemed a solid mass of gray-white now turned partly transparent. Jake could see through the snow, could see countless tiny snowflakes coming down, but could also see what they came down *through*. What had been nothingness suddenly became something. A space.

Within this space rose the mountain, not just before them, but above them, a great shape looming half visible through the falling snow. Jake saw rough white streaks that must have been snow-filled gullies on a cliff. He saw a relatively smooth lower slope and a much more jagged upper slope. He saw what must have been boulders jutting from the slope. What he couldn't see, however, was the summit. Too many clouds swept over Mount Remington's upper reaches to reveal the top. And even as he watched, the clouds shifted, the snow intensified, and most of the mountain disappeared.

Jake glanced at his sister. Danielle was staring off toward the mountain. What, he wondered, was she thinking? Did she really doubt they could climb Mount Remington? Did she really think they'd get killed? Or did she agree with him that they might succeed? He wanted to know what she thought. He wanted her to say everything would be okay.

Then Danielle did something Jake wasn't expecting. She reached over and hugged him. Her motions caught him off guard; for a moment he lost his balance and nearly stumbled. He reached out to her then and hugged her, too. He hugged her partly to keep from toppling over but partly, Jake realized, just because he needed to hug her. They stood like that, arms awkwardly around each other, for a long moment. Neither of them spoke. The only sound came from the hiss of snow on their coats and faces.

For the first time Jake started to worry that they'd never get out of there alive. The longer Danielle stayed quiet, the more scared Jake felt. Yet he understood just then that if they had any chance at all of surviving, they were each other's—and their parents'—only hope.

Before either of them could chicken out, Jake pulled away from Danielle and started down toward the valley and the mountain beyond.

THIRTEEN

▲▲

THEY SLID DOWN A SNOWY hillside. It was easy. Even in deep snow—deep enough that it boiled up around their legs as they pushed through it—Danielle hardly had to work at all. The long slide reminded her of how much fun the ski season would be that winter.

"Yeeee-ha!" Jake yelled as he followed her down, lashing the side of an imaginary bucking bronco.

Both of them made it to the bottom without falling. Then, staggering about in drifts again, they both flopped over into the snow.

Danielle struggled up and dusted herself off. "Whoa!" she exclaimed. "That was great." She reached out to help Jake up, but he refused her assistance.

They stood there looking around. Across from them rose an odd mass, dark gray and fuzzy-looking in the snowfall, spread out horizontally.

"What's this?" Jake asked.

"Beats me."

"I guess we'd better have a look."

What they'd seen wasn't a forest, exactly; instead, it was an expanse of branches growing right out of the ground, branches forming a tangle as thick and complex as treetops but without the lower limbs and trunks. Brush? Brambles? Danielle didn't know what to call them. All she knew was that these plants grew in thickets covering the ground from left to right as far as she could see.

First they tried to get around by heading off to the left. The thickets went on so far, however, that Danielle and Jake soon gave up and doubled back to the right. Once again they found themselves blocked. When they reached a gap in the wall of branches—a doorway in the wall—Danielle saw no alternative but to go through it.

Immediately they found themselves in a maze. The snow was deep, almost as deep as what they'd found earlier on the road. Yet the thickets caused more problems than the snow: lots of thin, cold branches thrashed them across the face with almost every step. Worse yet, they couldn't see where they were going. The bushes grew close together, forming narrow tunnels that reminded Danielle of an English garden maze she'd seen once in a photograph. People would enter the maze, wander about among its hedges, and get lost so easily that many of them would end up shouting for help to get out. She felt like that now. But there was no one beyond the maze—no one to tell them where to go.

"Are you sure we can get through this?" she asked.

Danielle heard Jake answer but couldn't understand him—he was a few paces ahead with his back to her.

Then some branches Jake was passing jiggled enough to loosen a big mass of snow. Danielle looked up just in time for it to tumble down on her.

"Watch out, would you?" Danielle shouted. But the faceful of snow wasn't what bothered her. What really worried Danielle was the possibility that they were already lost. No matter what direction they turned, all she saw was bushes and snow. Trying to follow the contour of the land didn't help much, for they were on the low ground between the hillside and the mountain. And the bushes grew tall enough to block their view in every direction.

Jake slipped and fell before he could grab some branches for support.

Danielle rushed ahead to help him. Then at once she fell, too.

They forced themselves up but sat there panting for a long time.

"I don't know if I can keep this up," Jake said at last.

"We have to," Danielle told him.

"Sure—but how?"

"Just a little longer. I'm sure we'll find our way out."

Danielle and Jake pushed their way through the brush and slogged through the snow but still couldn't feel sure of where they were. The passages angling off in different directions looked more and more alike. When the snow came down hard, they couldn't see anything at all. More than once Danielle thought they'd worked their way forward, then suddenly realized that she and Jake had doubled back and crossed paths with their own footprints.

"This is the pits!" Danielle screamed suddenly, kicking a thick bundle of branches. At once great heaps of snow tumbled down on her head and shoulders.

"Stop it," Jake said.

"I hate this!"

"I'm not so crazy about it, either."

"I feel like a needle in a haystack!" She almost kicked out again but held off. Her neck burned from the snow sifting down past her collar.

It took a while for Danielle to notice Jake. An odd, far-off look had come over his face.

"That's it," he said quietly.

"That's what?"

"A needle."

"What needle?" she asked.

"A compass needle."

Danielle couldn't figure out what he meant. "What compass? We don't have a compass."

"I know," Jake said.

"So what are you telling me?"

"What I'm telling you is—if we don't *have* a compass, let's *make* one."

"Make one? How?"

Jake didn't answer. He was already rummaging through his pack to find what he needed.

Danielle glanced at her watch. Eight-fifty. How much more time could they afford to waste?

By the time Jake finished pulling things out and choosing what he wanted, he'd laid out a bizarre array of odds and ends. A cork. His pocketknife. A thermos of hot cocoa. Mom's travel sewing kit. The little magnetic box that Dad used to hide a set of car keys for the Blazer. Jake proclaimed, "Ta-da!"

"I don't get it," Danielle said.

"It's what we need."

"For a compass?"

"You got it."

Danielle poked at the various things with her right index finger. "This better be good."

First Jake took Dad's Hide-a-Key and turned it upside down. There was a big black magnet plainly visible on the bottom. Then, removing a needle from Mom's sewing kit, Jake held one end; moving slowly, he drew the needle over the magnet fifteen or twenty times. Danielle felt more and more restless as she watched. Just when she was about to object, though, Jake said, "Here—hold this," and handed her the needle. She took it carefully. Jake then picked up the pocketknife, grabbed the cork, and cut off a slice about a quarter of an inch thick. He took the needle from Danielle, poked it into the side of the cork, and used the side of the knife's blade to shove it all the way through.

"Just what we need," Danielle said. "A slice of cork with a needle stuck through it sideways."

Jake ignored her. "Now the best part."

Holding the thermos, he unscrewed the cap and set it upside down. The cap became a cup. Then he unscrewed the stopper and poured the cup half full of cocoa. Steam rose at once from the cup, and the air filled with the delicious aroma of hot chocolate.

Danielle wondered for a moment if her brother had gone crazy. Then, watching him pick up the cork-and-needle thing, she understood. "You're going to *float* it—"

"—to make the compass," Jake said, finishing her sentence. He set the cork-and-needle on the cocoa's surface, where it floated, wavering and trembling.

"Does it work?" Danielle asked, feeling nervous. She glanced around. The snow was coming down hard again. "What's supposed to happen?"

"We magnetized the needle with Dad's Hide-a-Key.

The cork rests so lightly on the liquid that the needle can align itself with the earth's magnetic field." Cupping his hands over the cocoa, Jake peered into the viewfinder his fingers made. He watched in silence for a long time.

Danielle watched her brother till she couldn't stand it anymore. "Let me have a look," she demanded.

Smiling, Jake leaned back. "See for yourself."

Danielle took a turn cupping her hands over the cocoa. When she looked in, she saw the needle wavering slightly but pointing steadily in one direction—a direction far different from where she'd thought north should be.

"According to the map, Mount Remington is east of us," Jake said. "East is always at a right angle to north, so there's where we have to go." He gestured off to one side.

"You're sure?" Danielle asked.

"You saw the compass yourself," Jake replied. Then he plucked out the cork-and-needle thing, raised the cup in his other hand, said, "Cheers," and drank the cocoa.

His actions annoyed Danielle—Jake was always trying to be so cool—but the sight of him drinking cocoa got the best of her. "Let me have some," she told him abruptly.

"Why not?" Jake responded. He poured cocoa into the cup. Then, reaching into the lunch bag that Mom had given them, he added, "Here—have a granola bar, too. We should keep our strength up."

Half an hour later, after pouring more cocoa, checking the compass again, and working their way through the maze of brush, Danielle thought the bushes around them looked smaller than they'd looked earlier. Soon the bushes were less than shoulder high.

"I think we're out." Danielle stopped, glanced around, then went ahead quickly.

The bushes were now so short that Danielle could see right over them. And what she saw—straight ahead and looming far higher than seemed possible—was an expanse of something gray and white.

"The mountain!" Danielle shouted.

Jake rushed over. He looked past her, then shoved both fists in the air and jumped as high as he could. "Yes!"

They didn't even stop to rest before heading up.

FOURTEEN

▲▲

JAKE COULDN'T SEE WHAT HE and Danielle were climbing. The mountain itself rose somewhere beyond, but new flurries hid it almost completely. All they saw were the snow-covered rocks right in front of them and the grainy white air all around. Yet Jake felt pleased to be there. So pleased, in fact, that he could scarcely control himself as he scrambled upward.

"Slow down!" Danielle shouted from not far behind.

Jake felt amused by these words. Danielle the jock was pleading for an easier pace! "What's the matter," he called back, "can't you keep up?"

In just a few big strides Danielle caught up with him. "Listen to me," she blurted, sounding angry. "This isn't a race."

"So who's racing?"

"You're acting like *you* are."

Jake tried to laugh at her, but he was panting too hard. He managed to say, "Nah—going fast just feels good."

Danielle caught him by the sleeve, stopped short, and nearly toppled him over.

"Jake," she said, then faltered, catching her breath. "We have to pace ourselves. We've got a long ways to go."

"Get your hands off me." Jake tried tugging free of her grip.

"Not till you promise me something."

"What."

"We have to stay together. And work together."

"Come on—"

"This isn't a contest."

The more Danielle badgered him, the more Jake wanted to get going. "All right," he told Danielle, "I hear you." Jake headed off again. He knew Danielle was right. Just as the cross-country coach had always told him and the other runners: if you sprint at the start, you'll crawl to the finish line. Jake didn't really disagree with his sister. Still, he didn't appreciate her nagging him. She must have been parroting her Mountain Mastery pals.

Even the thought of that place put Jake on edge. As if Danielle weren't already conceited enough about her athletic prowess, she went off to the Rockies that summer and came back even more self-impressed. At Mountain Mastery she conquered the wilderness! Swung from ropes! Caught fish with her bare hands! Ate rocks for breakfast! Hung by her eyebrows from cliffs! Leaped from peak to peak! Jake was sick to death of hearing about Mountain Mastery.

Yet even while resenting his sister's pride in what she'd done that summer, Jake knew that both he and Danielle now depended on her knowledge. What would they face in climbing Mount Remington? He couldn't even guess. So far the task had been easier than what he'd expected. Maybe this climb wouldn't end up more difficult than a long, cold hike. Yet he wasn't so sure. The TV program about Mount Remington had shown scenery far different from what he saw now. Cliffs. Jagged outcroppings of rock. A few metal huts huddled together at the summit. No matter how much he hated hearing Danielle's stories about scaling peaks and surviving in the wilderness, Jake could only hope that his sister knew as much as she thought she did.

That first push upward wasn't so bad. As Jake had hoped, the winds swept Mount Remington free of snow—or, if not quite free, then at least freer than on the low-lying areas he and Danielle had struggled through earlier. The surface underfoot was solid beneath what little snow clung to the rocks. The mountain's angle wasn't very steep. Jake found it hard to believe that they wouldn't make good progress.

Even the weather didn't bother them. They felt cold at first but soon less so: the effort itself warmed them. The task seemed almost pleasant. Both Jake and Danielle relaxed, stopped hassling each other, and even kidded around a bit. At the rate they were going, they'd surely reach the top in an hour or two. Help would be on the way soon afterward.

FIFTEEN
▲▲

"LOOK! DANIELLE, LOOK!"

She turned to see what Jake was hollering about. Standing just a few yards downhill from Danielle, he faced away from her and away from the mountain. The storm had eased. The air suddenly emptied of snow. Looking out from Mount Remington, Danielle could now see the valley and the peaks forming its other side.

"What is it?" she shouted back. The wind snatched the words out of her mouth.

Jake swung about to glance up at her; then he motioned toward the valley.

"The Blazer!"

Danielle peered down the slope, scanned the snowy terrain below, and tried to see what he meant. She saw the mountainside dropping beneath them. She saw the low area at the mountain's base and the maze of brush that she and Jake had struggled through. She saw the hill above the brush and, running along the hill's long crest, the snow-covered road. She saw the scraggly forest beyond. But the Blazer?

"Right!" she exclaimed, suddenly catching sight of the family car. "I see it!"

She couldn't believe how high they'd come already. They must have gained almost a thousand feet of altitude. Where did that put them on the mountain? She couldn't even guess. She wanted to think they were halfway up, but there was no way of knowing without an altimeter or a map. In such bad weather, too, even the use of instruments wouldn't have provided a clear sense of their location. But they must have been halfway up, she told herself. They couldn't possibly have made all this effort and not be that high. Surely they'd reach the top within an hour. The thought thrilled her.

Just then she had another thought. Suddenly alarmed, Danielle peered down through the space between the mountain and the Blazer far below. "You think they're all right?" she murmured.

Jake didn't seem to grasp the words. "What's that?" he called back.

Danielle shouted, "I said, I hope they're all right!"

She just couldn't tell. Danielle saw no signs of activity down there: no one moving about, no exhaust from the car, no lights flashing. A deep chill seeped into her bones. She imagined Mom and Dad huddled together, wrapped in the quilts but still shivering, Flash nuzzled against them, the Blazer's engine silent and still because all the gas was gone. . . . How long could they fend off the cold? How long could they withstand the effects of their injuries? Danielle felt sick at the thought of what Mom and Dad must have been going through.

She turned to look up the mountainside. All she saw was the great pile of white-dusted rocks fading below.

"Let's get going," she told Jake, then headed up again without waiting for him.

Danielle and Jake plodded up much as before. Danielle could see the mountain changing, though, as they proceeded upward. What had been relatively small chunks of rock underfoot—chunks the size of books, pillows, basketballs, and loaves of bread—had grown much larger. Many of the chunks weren't even chunks now: more like slabs and boulders. Some looked about the size of TVs or suitcases. Others were as big as sofas. Danielle and Jake weren't climbing *up* some of these rocks but *around* them. The snow covering them made the rocks slippery. Time after time Danielle found herself sliding down surfaces that otherwise wouldn't have given her any trouble. Once or twice she slipped so fast that she lost her balance and barely caught herself as she toppled forward. Luckily, the wind blew hard enough that much of the snow never stuck to the upper surfaces—it just accumulated on the far side of each rock. Even so, the task of climbing got more and more difficult.

The difficulty soon brought back all her doubts. Danielle couldn't help wondering if this plan would really work out. It wasn't just that the climb might be too difficult; she didn't even feel sure about the goal itself.

"Are you positive there's a weather station up there?" she asked Jake. "I haven't spotted anything the least bit like a weather station."

Jake shrugged. "You can't see it from here. It must be right over the top."

"But you know it's there."

"It's there, okay? It's there."

"You're positive?"

"Positive."

"*Absolutely* positive?"

"Danielle, it's there. It's *got* to be there."

These words stunned Danielle. "What do you mean, it's *got* to be there?"

"Just what I said."

"Before you said it's there. Now you're saying it's *got* to be there."

They argued a while longer. Danielle got more and more annoyed; Jake got more and more defensive.

Neither of them seemed willing to admit it, but both felt more and more frightened about the situation they'd got themselves into.

Then, abruptly, Jake said, "Over there," and pointed out something to the west.

Danielle thought he must have been trying to distract her, to change the subject and brush her off. When she looked west, though, she saw at once what he meant.

Big, dark clouds were massing off to the west, sweeping toward Mount Remington, and blotting out the other peaks and valleys one by one as they approached. Within a few minutes, the air turned white again.

SIXTEEN
▲▲

Jake had stumbled a few times before he realized that something other than snow and unstable rocks had made him clumsy. He felt so hungry that his legs started shaking. Sometimes that happened to him. The doctor called it hypoglycemia: low blood sugar. Now and then he got that way at school, too, especially at gym class. Once he got so shaky that he passed out. As if the jocks needed any more reason to make fun of him! Shaky Jakey, they called him afterward. So now here he was, scrambling up a mountain in the middle of a blizzard with his head pounding and his legs turning to rubber.

"Danielle, I need lunch."

His sister had been trailing him just then, having let him go ahead for a while. Now she looked up at him with an expression that Jake figured was either annoyance or puzzlement. "I couldn't hear you," she called up to him.

"Lunch."

"What about it?"

"I'm hungry."

Danielle stopped, staring as if he'd said he wanted to take a bath. *"Now?* It's only ten-thirty-five."

He decided to meet her head-on. "I bet they taught you something about food at Mountain Mastery. Keeping your strength up, maintaining your stamina, all that stuff?"

"Okay, okay," she said, "you're right. We should take a break. No use running out of steam. If you want lunch, let's have lunch."

They found a big rock to huddle against. The wind shot over the top, dusting them constantly with snow, but at least the cold couldn't stab straight through their coats. Compared to being on the slope, this was almost cozy.

Jake pulled off his pack, dumped it on a rock, tugged it open, and began to take things out. The rope lay right on top. Some extra socks did, too. Most of the tools rested farther down—he'd put them there on purpose, hoping to avoid rearranging things more than necessary. He found the bag of Flash's dog food and lifted it out.

He could hardly wait for what he'd do next.

Flattening his ski cap till it rested on his head like a beret, Jake nodded curtly at his sister. *"Bonjour, Mademoiselle.* And what may we serve you today?"

Danielle glanced at him, then away. *"Don't,"* she said.

"May I suggest ze Doggie Dinnair?"

"Jake, please don't."

"It eez ze specialty of ze house."

"Stop it, would you?" she blurted, though she couldn't keep back a smile. "This is bad enough without you trying to be cute."

"Or perhaps Mademoiselle would prefer ze Crittair Frittairs?"

"Don't gross me out."

"Or may I—"

"Jake, I'm warning you!"

"It's all we've got," he said just then, dropping the accent. "We ate the granola bars and drank the cocoa, so it's this or nothing."

"I'm not eating dog food."

"Danielle, it's nutritionally complete."

"Don't start."

"Did you know that the pet food companies make their stuff suitable for human consumption?" Jake asked. When Danielle didn't respond, he added, "You know why? Because people end up eating about ten or twenty percent of the pet food sold. Isn't that incredible?"

Danielle said nothing. She just stared at her lap.

"Ten or twenty percent!" Jake exclaimed.

At last Danielle managed to ask, "Why would anyone want to eat *dog* food?"

"Because they don't have any choice. Because they can't afford anything else. You know—poor people."

She didn't look reassured by what Jake was saying.

"So the companies have to make it safe enough for humans. And nutritious enough, too."

Danielle said nothing.

"Did you know," he continued, "that Alaskan bush pilots sometimes stow bags of dog chow on their planes? Fifty-pound bags? That way, if they crash-land somewhere, they'll have some real concentrated food to keep them alive till someone rescues them."

By now Danielle was getting angry. "Jake, do me a favor. If you want to eat the stuff, go ahead. Eat all you want. Eat my share, for all I care. But would you please stop *talking* about it?"

Jake felt put off by Danielle's words. He was just trying to be helpful, he told himself. He wanted to cheer her up. But if that's what she wanted—well, that was fine with him.

So he reached into the bag, tugged it open, and pulled out a handful of Critter Fritters. The odor caught his attention at once: warm and moist. It smelled a bit fishy but not at all unpleasant. It reminded him of times and places he couldn't quite identify. Maybe the New England coast a few years back. Maybe Fisherman's Wharf in San Francisco. Maybe his own house: one of Dad's specialties was a fish chowder he'd learned to make in Maine. All Jake knew was that the scent made him feel a sudden twinge of longing. He didn't want to be stuck on this mountain. He didn't want to be mucking around in the snow. He wanted to be home again; he wanted to be warm and cozy; he wanted to be seated at the table in the kitchen with his family, eating food hot from the stove. . . .

"Well, Pierre, how's the specialty of the house?"

Danielle's voice brought him back to reality. Jake found himself sitting there on the western slope of Mount Remington, his sister right beside him, a handful of Critter Fritters clutched in his right hand. He looked at the dog food in his palm. Suddenly the little lumps didn't look at all appetizing.

"Well?" she asked.

With his left hand Jake picked up three lumps and, without hesitating, popped them into his mouth like peanuts. He chewed as quickly as possible. He swallowed.

The taste wasn't half bad. A bit oily. Tougher than he'd expected. Sort of gritty. Not really unpleasant, though. The truth was, Jake felt too hungry to care. Without answering Danielle's question he popped more nuggets into his mouth, chewed them, swallowed, popped in more, chewed, and swallowed again. Pretty soon he'd eaten the whole handful.

He turned to his sister. He smiled.

Before he could speak, Danielle said, "Don't you dare tell me anything in French."

Leaning close, as if to whisper something in her ear, Jake said, *"Woof."*

SEVENTEEN
▲▲

FORTIFIED BY A HEARTY MEAL OF Flash's dog food—even Danielle had eaten some— they started up again. Sometimes Danielle went first; sometimes Jake did. They didn't go very fast, and both of them got winded more quickly than before, but at least they made steady progress. Danielle found it easy to believe that they'd reach the top pretty soon.

The thought of getting there pleased her but also surprised her. To think that Jake's loony idea would actually work out! The climb hadn't been so difficult after all. They hadn't even needed to use any of the skills Danielle had learned that summer. She felt a twinge of disappointment when she thought about reaching the top so easily—she hadn't been able to show what *she* could do. Jake would be the one whose cleverness would shine. Jake would get all the credit.

During one of their brief rests, while they sat with their backs to the mountain, Jake suddenly looked as if he might have spotted something below. Danielle turned to gaze down there, too. "What is it?" she asked excitedly.

"I have an idea," Jake told her.

"What did you see?"

Jake wasn't even looking around. "Nothing. I just had this great idea. When we get up there and reach the station—you know, at the top—let's pound on the door."

Danielle's disappointment turned to annoyance. "Of *course* we'll pound on the door. What did you think we'll do, just wait till someone wanders out to admire the view?"

"No, listen—I'm not done. We'll pound on the door. Then, when they pull it open, let's hold out our empty packs like grocery bags and yell, 'Trick or treat!' "

Danielle stared at Jake. "I can't believe you'd do that," she said. "I can't believe you're even *talking* about doing it."

Jake forced a laugh. "Don't you think that'd be great? Just imagine the look on their faces!"

"It's an incredibly dumb idea."

"No, really—let's do it."

"We're dragging our butts up this mountain, Mom and Dad are freezing to death, and you're cooking up practical jokes!"

He looked upset. "It doesn't hurt anything, does it?"

"It sure doesn't help much."

"You're such a spoilsport," Jake said, folding his arms across his chest and pulling his knees up.

Danielle didn't even feel like answering him.

That's what I can never understand about Jake, Danielle thought. What makes him likable is exactly what drives me up the wall. He's intelligent but has no common sense. He can design a working mousetrap from paper clips and rubber bands but can't remember to tie his bootlaces. He can improvise a compass out of a needle, a cork, and a cup of cocoa, but even in an emergency his brain is busy inventing gags to play when we reach the summit. *If* we reach the summit.

Fear welled up in her again. The climb had gone so easily that Danielle kept forgetting about the uncertainties ahead. Not just the climb itself. She could tell that Mount Remington was growing steeper, but steepness wasn't what worried Danielle at that particular moment. Something else, something more basic, nagged at her.

Would they find the weather station at the top?

Or would they find nothing but a mound of rocks and snow?

Was this climb Jake's most brilliant idea?

Or was it just another of his harebrained schemes?

She didn't know—and that's what scared her most of all.

EIGHTEEN

▲▲

MOUNT REMINGTON GOT steeper and steeper. Soon it was so steep that Jake felt more and more uneasy with each step he took. What had seemed a little like scrambling up a huge ruined staircase now felt more like scaling a rough, sloping stone wall. An enormous wall. A wall in which the stones were slippery with snow and sometimes unstable. Time after time Jake stepped onto stones that tipped under his weight. Now and then stones came loose, tumbled downward, and smashed to bits on the mountainside. Luckily, he managed to keep his grip. He didn't fall. But each step left Jake feeling uncertain, and looking down made his stomach flutter with a sensation halfway between nausea and pain. He knew that even the smallest mistake would send him crashing down just like those rocks.

Jake watched his sister climbing slightly ahead of him and to his right. He couldn't believe how easy Danielle made it look. She was out of breath, yet she didn't seem to be working hard at all. She never lost her balance. She hadn't fallen even once. She boosted herself from one foothold to the next without much effort. Although Jake knew that the climb's success depended on his sister's skill, he resented Danielle anyway.

Maybe it's all because of Mountain Mastery, Jake told himself. Danielle had never even set foot on a mountain till that summer. Now she acted like she'd been climbing all her life. Of course Danielle had always had been good at sports. She'd been a gymnast for as long as Jake could remember, and she had a whole shelfful of prizes from gymnastic competitions. In middle school she'd taken up track; within the first year she became one of the team's fastest sprinters. She'd joined the swim team as well. She also played other sports just for fun. Field hockey. Softball. And now mountain climbing.

What bothered Jake wasn't really that Danielle did so well at all these sports. He didn't hold that against her. She had a right to be good at sports, he told himself, and a right to enjoy them. But did she have to rub it in? Danielle never let Jake forget her athletic prowess. It wasn't that she said anything outright.

What she did was indirect. How she smiled at him when he stumbled . . . How she grew impatient while trying to teach him flips at the local pool . . . How she said, "Well, you did your best," when he'd struck out at a neighborhood softball game . . . Danielle made it hard for him to feel comfortable with her abilities; she made it even harder for Jake to feel comfortable with his own. Jake knew he wasn't nearly as good an athlete as Danielle. In some ways that bothered him, but in other ways he didn't care. He knew he was good in his own way. He enjoyed cross-country running and bicycle touring, since both sports emphasized concentration and stamina. Danielle was such a jock, though, that he'd always felt caught in her shadow. As a result, Jake had generally tried staying clear of her in the situations where she could show off her skills.

Now here he was, stuck on a mountain with her!

"I don't think we can keep going like this."

Jake wasn't sure what to think when Danielle spoke these words. "You mean we should quit?" he asked, sounding surprised.

"No, dummy," she said. "I mean we can't just climb unprotected."

"What do you mean, *unprotected?*"

"You know—without equipment. At least not without a rope."

They had reached a kind of shelf set into the mountainside, a place where the steepness let up briefly before angling upward again. There Jake and Danielle reached the first good resting place they'd found in half an hour. They sat, took off their packs, and caught their breath.

"So you think we should use some gear?"

"That's what I'm getting at."

"Don't we need some sort of hook?" Jake asked, gazing up the mountain.

"Hook?" Danielle just stared at him.

"You know," Jake went on. "A hook to throw up there and catch on the rocks."

"That's not how you do it."

"I saw some guys climb that way on TV. They had a hook on a rope. They'd throw the hook up the cliff till it caught on something. Then they'd climb the rope."

"You'd get yourself killed that way," Danielle said.

"But these guys on TV—"

"This isn't TV."

"I know it's not."

"So don't be such a nerd. You don't climb by throwing a hook and climbing the rope."

Jake gestured impatiently. "Then how *do* you climb?"

"You climb. You climb the best you can."

He flung his hands up in exasperation. "I don't get it! You climb—great! So what's the rope for, anyway?"

"It's sort of like a safety belt. You don't climb the rope itself, you use it to catch you if you fall."

"I give up!" Jake yelled. "This doesn't make sense!"

Danielle reached out and grabbed him by the arm. "Listen to me—I'm not trying to give you a hard time. Just let me explain, okay?"

Jake shrugged. He knew he ought to listen. Danielle *did* know more than Jake did about the task before them. No matter how much she got on his nerves, he decided he had to pay attention.

"Here's what you do," she went on. "First rule: only one of us climbs at any one time. The second person protects the other by using what's called a belay."

"A what?"

"A belay. It's what I compared to a safety belt."

"I've never heard of anyone climbing with a safety belt," Jake said. An image floated into his head: a mountain climber strapped to a cliff like a window washer.

"Would you just hear me out?" Danielle asked, now almost pleading. "I'm trying to explain."

The sense of urgency in her voice was unmistakable. "Okay, okay—go ahead," Jake told her.

After a moment's hesitation, Danielle started in again. "I don't mean a safety belt like a seat belt. More like a lifeline. It's sort of—maybe I should just show you." And with those words she reached out to her brother, pulled the towrope from his pack, and uncoiled it. Then she wound the free end several times around his waist and tied a complicated knot to secure it. She tugged it twice to make sure it was safe. "Theoretically," she went on, "you should be wearing what's called a harness—something to distribute the force if you fall."

"I wish you wouldn't talk so much about falling."

"But that's the whole point, isn't it—falling?"

"I guess so."

Danielle said, "Watch." She took the rest of the rope, gathered it into a coil again, and dumped the coil at her feet. She looped a length of rope around a big rock, then passed a length around her torso, pulled it tighter, and tied a knot right at waist level. Then Danielle sat in the snow next to the rock. The coil lay in the snow beside her. Holding the rope in both hands—the end connected to Jake now in her right hand, the end passing down to the coil now in her left—she said, "Lean off the edge."

"*What?*" Jake asked, not sure if he'd heard right.

"Lean off the edge."

"You're crazy."

"Just do it."

He peered down. The cliff looked much steeper now. Even climbing back down would have been dangerous. If he fell, he'd break his neck.

"Trust me," Danielle said.

"I trust you," Jake responded. "I just don't particularly want to die young."

Danielle said, "Look. This isn't quite like going for a Sunday stroll, is it? I'll admit it's risky."

"So then why—"

"Because it's less risky than *not* doing it. And that's why climbers do it."

"Danielle—"

"Maybe it'll save your neck. Maybe it'll save mine."

"Danielle, let me just—"

"How about if you stop being so stubborn?"

"I'm not being stubborn," Jake protested.

"You are."

"I'm not."

"You think you know everything."

"No, I don't. Not about *this*." Jake motioned toward the rope around his waist. "How could I? I haven't been to Mountain Mastery. I'm not Superjock."

For a while they fell silent. The wind whistled over the mountain and fluttered against their coats. Jake stood there feeling bad about what he'd said, but he couldn't think of anything to soften the words or take them back.

Danielle sat there with the rope in both hands.

"Sorry," Jake said.

"Don't call me a jock, okay?"

"But you *are* a jock."

"No I'm not."

"You *are*."

"Look, I don't like that word."

"Well, I don't like being called a nerd."

"But you *are* one."

"Danielle—"

"Let's make a deal, okay? If you don't call me a jock, I won't call you a nerd."

Jake stood there a moment without speaking. Then, surprising himself as well as Danielle, he said, "All right, all right—let's get this over with."

Danielle perked up at once. "Okay," she answered. "Just lean back."

So he did. Jake shifted his weight, leaned back, and tilted away from the mountainside.

This is it, he thought. I'm dead.

A few inches of rope slid out of the coil, through Danielle's left hand, around her back, and through her right hand. Jake could feel his body tilting so far that he expected to fall backward, headfirst, down the cliff. Then Danielle brought her left fist—the fist now tightly clutching the coil side of the rope—and shoved the fist against her right hip. At once the rope stopped sliding. It tightened against her back. The length running from Danielle's right hand to Jake's torso tightened as well and stopped Jake from tilting back any farther than he had already. He didn't fall.

"Whoa!" he exclaimed in amazement and fear.

"See?" Danielle asked. "It works."

Jake couldn't believe it. Danielle was right: the belay *did* work. But all he could think about just then was regaining his balance. Crouching, Jake shifted his weight forward, reached out to the cliff with both hands, then scrambled back to where Danielle sat before him.

Once he'd caught his breath he said, "So that's a belay. Great. But how does that help me if I *really* fall?"

"The same way."

"Won't I pull you off the cliff?"

"Not likely."

"Why not?"

"Because when I'm on belay I'll be anchored—" Then she caught herself short. "Jake, it's too complicated to explain." She glanced nervously at her watch. "It's almost eleven. We can't spare the time. Let's just head up again—I'll explain as we go."

"Danielle, I need to know," Jake protested.

"Trust me, okay?"

"Danielle—"

"If we take any longer, we'll never get there. You just have to trust me."

NINETEEN
▲▲

DANIELLE HOPED THEY MIGHT climb Mount Remington by relying only on the rope for assistance. She still didn't feel convinced that they could improvise climbing hardware out of the tools Jake had brought along. Danielle's Mountain Mastery instructors had stressed over and over that each piece of equipment has its own specific function. You don't use an ice screw as a piton. You don't use chocks, nuts, cams, and other kinds of hardware interchangeably. You don't use an ice ax as a pick or use a pick as a mountaineering hammer. There's a little room for improvisation, but not much, and in any case you'd better know what you're doing. It was one thing for Jake to make a toy airplane out of paper cups and soda straws, Danielle told herself. It would be quite another for him to fake climbing hardware out of screwdrivers and carpenter's hammers. If they could only keep going as they had been already, though, using the rope just in case . . .

She worried more about Jake than about herself. Danielle could climb this slope without too much difficulty; it was steep but not so steep that she felt in great danger. Even as the going got trickier, Danielle hadn't slipped even once. But Jake was another story. He'd kept up better than she'd expected, but he still climbed like someone who'd never done it before. From time to time he slipped. Earlier, on the mountain's lower reaches, the slips didn't matter. He'd stumble, he'd catch himself, he'd head up again. Now there was no margin for error. Even a relatively small mistake could send him tumbling down the cliff. Danielle couldn't let him take that chance.

This is why they proceeded as they did. Tied together by the rope, Danielle always went up first while Jake waited below. Jake, taking his turn as the belayer, played out the rope as Danielle climbed. Danielle held off explaining what she hoped her brother wouldn't notice: that his role as belayer didn't really serve much purpose. If Danielle were to fall while climbing above him, the rope in Jake's hands wouldn't help her, since she hadn't linked the rope to the cliff with any of the protective devices that climbers would ordinarily have used. Danielle would fall just as far as if Jake weren't holding the belay rope in the first place. What was the point, though, of telling him? He was nervous enough already.

When Jake took his turns climbing, though, the situation was completely different. Danielle, seated firmly and bracing her feet against a rock, pulled in the rope as her brother worked his way up. He did pretty well—better than she'd thought he would. When Jake lost his footing, Danielle pulled the rope in her left hand against her chest so hard that she caught Jake before he'd dropped more than a few inches. He never fell far enough to suffer any harm. This had two big benefits. One was that he reached her safely time after time. The other was that the reassurance they both gained from this arrangement put Jake more at ease, so that he climbed more confidently and slipped less often.

Soon they'd gained another several hundred feet of altitude. The lower slopes of Mount Remington now lay far below—so far, in fact, that they seemed almost soft to the touch, more like pale leather than a rocky mountainside. The valley beyond faded in the snowfall. Danielle couldn't see the road, the forest, or the Blazer. Gazing outward, she found it hard to believe that there could be other people anywhere else on earth.

"You think Mom and Dad are okay?" asked Jake as they rested, leaning back against the mountain.

"I hope so," Danielle said. She kept thinking about her parents' injuries. It was hard to imagine them so badly hurt. It didn't seem possible—Mom and Dad with broken bones and banged-up joints. Even if they managed to get out of there, would they be all right?

"I wonder if they have any gas left."

Danielle didn't respond at first. She was thinking about her weekly tennis matches with Mom. Then she glanced at her watch. "It's a quarter to noon," she said, more to herself than to her brother. At once she regretted having spoken at all. Even a quick glance in his direction showed her that Jake was already up to something.

"Let's see now," said Jake. "We've been gone since about seven A.M., so we'll say five hours. The Blazer had maybe one-third of a tank left—"

"Jake."

He ignored her. He didn't even notice her. "—and the tank holds twenty gallons."

"Jake?"

"The big question is, What's the rate of consumption while the car is idling?"

"Jake!"

He jolted like someone wakened from a dream. "What?" he exclaimed, glancing up suddenly.

Danielle couldn't think of what to say. She wanted him to stop. She wanted him to ease up and not get so desperate to figure things out. Yet she realized just then that Jake was simply trying to reassure himself. He needed to do this. It was how he expressed his concern about Mom and Dad.

"What is it?" Jake asked her.

"Nothing," Danielle said.

Jake looked at her for a while, then gazed off toward the valley again. He said, "I hope they're okay."

During the next twenty minutes, Danielle and Jake climbed another hundred feet up the mountainside. It was hard work. Danielle could feel her muscles getting tired, and she knew that Jake was tired, too. The task got harder and harder as the nature of the cliff changed. Earlier, the rocks had been big: great slabs and boulders wedged on top of one another. Now the rocks seemed smaller, more like what they had encountered below: bits and pieces, chunks and fragments, everything piled together like a vast heap of broken crockery clacking and clattering underfoot. Danielle told herself that she should have been pleased with the changes, but she wasn't. The slope was much steeper than Mount Remington's lower reaches. She didn't feel comfortable here. She kept feeling things shift underfoot.

"Jake," she said suddenly.

"What is it?"

"I don't like this."

"Don't like what?"

"This place. These—conditions."

"It's better than dangling from a cliff."

"I'm not so sure." The longer she stood there, the more uncomfortable she felt.

Jake was on her left. Danielle was aware of him while they spoke, and now and then she glanced his way, but she felt so unstable that she didn't want to move too fast. She feared she might lose her balance. Something told her that Jake was in a better place than she was, however, so Danielle decided to work her way over to him.

"Jake—"

"What."

"Stay right where you are."

He must have detected something in her tone of voice. "What's wrong?" he asked.

"Nothing. At least not yet."

"Are you okay?"

"Listen to me. I want you to work your way closer to those big rocks. Slowly."

"Got it."

She didn't turn to face him again, but she could hear the crunch of his boots on the granite rubble. The noises grew complex: not the click-clack-clack of a few big rocks pushed about but instead the sputter and hiss of many small rocks starting to slide.

"Doing okay?" she called out.

"Fine."

"Are you there?"

"Almost."

Danielle was aware of Jake's motions beside her but still didn't feel safe turning. "Good," she said. "Now if you can, hook the rope around something. A big rock. One that's not just lying on the surface."

A few seconds passed. Danielle didn't hear anything, so she turned carefully, almost delicately, to her left. She could see Jake—his back was toward her—but she couldn't tell if he'd succeeded in doing what she'd asked.

A moment later Danielle knew something was wrong. It wasn't obvious, like having a rock crack off underfoot and send her falling. It was something quieter than that, something she almost couldn't identify. More of a feeling than an event. A feeling that something wasn't right. A feeling that no matter how huge this mountain may have been, it was far more delicate than it looked.

Danielle turned to her brother just then. Jake glanced back, aware of her alarm, maybe aware of his own, too, but looking just as puzzled as she felt.

"What's going on?" he asked.

"I don't know," she replied.

When she turned away, she understood. Danielle took a step, but it made no difference. The rock she stepped on—a rock bigger than a basketball—sank under the weight of her foot. She took another step and managed to make a little headway, but not much. The rocks shifted beneath her weight. No matter how carefully she stepped, her feet pushed the rocks downward as if shoving them into soft mud. Nothing happened fast. Nothing made much noise. She seemed to be climbing in slow motion: her foot rising and stepping into place, her muscles flexing to boost Danielle up onto the rock, then the rock sinking. No matter how hard she worked, she ended up no higher than before. And all along she heard a peculiar sound, too, a dry, brittle sound like that of cloth starting to tear.

Once again Danielle glanced toward her brother. Jake wasn't more than ten feet off, yet he seemed miles away.

"Jake?" she called out, surprised by the fear in her own voice.

"Stay still," he told her.

"I can't." Even as she spoke, Danielle could feel the rocks shifting steadily.

"Stay totally still."

She was aware of Jake easing to his left, where some large rocks—boulders, really—lay embedded among the smaller ones. Would they be more solid than the rest? Danielle wasn't so sure. The whole mountainside felt as treacherous as quicksand. But she could tell what Jake had in mind: if he could just reach the boulders, they'd have at least a chance at hanging on.

Just then Danielle felt the rocks beneath her give way. They didn't slide all of a sudden, just fast enough that she had to scramble to avoid going down with them. Letting out a little cry, she grabbed a rock right ahead of her, a rock bigger than a large watermelon, for support. Yet that rock, too, came loose. It would have rolled right into her if Danielle hadn't moved fast, scrambing onto it and over it and letting it tumble away underfoot. Then more rocks came down, sliding slowly at first, none of them in a hurry but all of them big enough that Danielle had no choice but to jump out of the way. Smaller stuff came down, too—chunks, blocks, bits. And at her back Danielle could hear all this stuff picking up speed: a complicated clatter that sounded like fire-crackers going off, dozens of firecrackers, then hun-dreds, then thousands at once.

She was too scared to scream. All she could do was struggle to avoid going down, too. The whole moun-tain seemed to be falling apart right underneath her. Danielle groped at the rocks sliding toward her, dodged the ones that came down fast and climbed over the ones that came down slowly. No matter how hard she struggled, she didn't get anywhere. She felt like someone running up a down escalator. Soon the whole mountainside seemed to be shifting at once, and Danielle could feel herself going down with it.

Yet as she slid, quickly out of control, Danielle discovered that the fear she felt wasn't just what she would have expected. She felt afraid—more afraid than she'd ever felt before—but not just for herself. For Jake, too, who would end up yanked down by Danielle's weight as she fell. And for her parents, huddled together far below in a frigid car.

TWENTY
▲▲

CLINGING TO A HUGE ROCK with all his might, Jake felt an almost irresistible force tug at his body. Something squeezed him hard around the waist. His spine ached. His fingers hurt so much he thought the skin would rip right off. All he wanted was to let go and release the forces tearing him apart. Yet something deep within him told Jake not to give up so easily. Better to struggle. Better to fight back no matter how bad the pain.

A memory floated into Jake's awareness: some other struggle, now long past. He could recall clinging to a flat surface then, too. Not rock, but wood. A dock of some sort? A pier? He could recall feeling cold then as well, and achy all over. . . .

The tugging at his waist grew so painful that it yanked him back into the present. Jake needed a few seconds to figure out what had happened. The last thing he remembered clearly was Danielle's voice ordering him to find safer ground. Jake hadn't understood the words just then, but her tone of voice had said it all. They were in big trouble. He'd obeyed. Jake had scrambled to the left. He'd tried to reach the boulders jutting up among the smaller, less stable rocks. He'd skittered about in a mixture of snow and fractured granite. Somehow he'd made it. Then, groping for safety, Jake had clutched at the nearest rock and hung on tight. That's when the force—the force he now understood was Danielle's weight tugging on the rope—had grasped him about the waist and nearly yanked him loose.

Jake didn't know how much longer he could hang on. The rope seemed ready to pull him apart, and he could feel sharp ridges of granite cutting deep into his flesh.

"Danielle!" Jake shouted. "Danielle!"

He waited for an answer.

All he heard was the hiss of the falling snow.

"Danielle!"

Still no answer.

Now something worse than pain shot through him: fear. Jake realized right then that Danielle might be hurt. How badly hurt? That depended on how far she'd fallen. He tried to glance over his shoulder but couldn't—even the least movement might make him

118

lose his grip. He shouted again instead: "Danielle!"

Once again he heard no answer.

A deep chill came over him. *Danielle is dead,* Jake told himself. The thought made him sick. He couldn't believe it but knew it might still be true. Otherwise why didn't she answer him? Why didn't she respond by some other means—tugging on the rope, if nothing else? The longer Jake thought about the situation, the more scared he felt. Thinking about Danielle down there—dangling from the rope or crumpled on the cliff—filled him with dread.

Yet it wasn't just Danielle he worried about. He realized at once what her fall meant about *him*. How long could Jake keep his grip on the rock? As soon as he let go, he'd tumble down, too. And of course that would leave Mom and Dad stuck down there in the Blazer, with no one aware of them and their predicament.

Then, just as Jake could feel his hands starting to slip, he heard a sound. It was faint—almost too faint to hear. By tilting his head slightly to the left, though, he managed to catch it better.

His own name.

He tried shouting but couldn't get his voice to work.

Again he heard his name, again faintly.

Now he managed to get the words out. *"Are! You! All! Right!"*

He waited, listening hard.

Nothing.

Maybe he'd heard only the snowfall, he told himself. Maybe the wind.

Then, during a lull, he heard something else, something unmistakable: *"Don't move!"*

Jake felt so excited that he almost lost his grip on the rock. The sound of those two words renewed his hope. He ignored his aching muscles. He clenched his fingers even harder against the rough granite beneath them.

No more words reached him for a while, but something better did: a sudden easing of the force that tugged so hard at Jake's body. It happened all at once. First he could barely hang on; then, suddenly, the weight was off. The rope fell limp against the back of his legs.

Jake crawled farther up onto the rock, collapsed, and lay there panting. The fingers of both hands throbbed as if badly burned. His whole body hurt. He couldn't remember having ever been so tired. Jake felt like someone who had barely reached the shore after having almost drowned.

He grew aware just then of some new sounds: scraping, hissing, and clattering sounds that grew louder with each passing moment. Jake forced himself up. He turned to look down the mountainside.

Danielle, working her way toward him, had just appeared from around the far side of the ridge.

* * *

She was clearly hurt. She wasn't moving right: slowly, awkwardly, far too carefully. She looked unsure, almost dazed. She was trembling hard. At least she kept coming up, though. Jake couldn't see anything that suggested she'd broken any bones. And even before she'd reached the rock, she smiled and gave Jake a thumbs-up signal.

Jake braced himself against a ridge on the boulder and reached down to help her up. Danielle reached back with her right hand. At first he almost toppled headfirst from the burden of her weight; then he shifted his position, clutched the rock with one hand, got a better grip on Danielle's wrist with the other, and pulled her to safety.

At once she collapsed and flopped belly-down on the rock. She lay there shaking and gasping for breath a long time.

He was shocked to see what a battering she'd taken. Her face was covered with lots of small cuts. He saw some bruises, too. "Are you all right?" Jake asked her when Danielle managed to sit up.

She looked dizzy and exhausted. "Yes. No. I think so," she said. Danielle reached up with one hand, touched her face, and looked at the blood on her fingertips. "How bad am I hurt?"

"You're pretty banged up," he said. Jake didn't know what else to say. "You think you broke any bones?"

121

Danielle shifted this way and that to see how well her muscles and joints worked. "I don't think so," she answered, "but I'm awfully sore." Then, without warning, she leaned close and hugged her brother.

Jake felt surprised but hugged her back.

"Thanks for helping me," Danielle said.

Jake couldn't think of what to say.

"You did just the right thing."

He said, "I didn't really do anything at all."

"Yes, you did."

"I mean, I didn't *plan* to. Or try to. I just fumbled around and got lucky."

"I don't care. You still did the right thing."

They stayed there only ten or fifteen minutes. Jake worried about Danielle—he thought she needed to rest a while longer—but Danielle protested and told him they needed to keep moving. It was almost one o'clock already. They didn't have any time to spare. The snow was coming down harder now; the wind was picking up. Danielle complained of feeling cold. Jake felt cold, too. Even eating more of Flash's dog food didn't do much to warm them up. Ultimately the cold was what tipped the balance. Nothing but resuming the climb would shake off the chill now seeping into Jake's and Danielle's flesh.

TWENTY-ONE

▲▲

EVEN BEFORE SHE STOPPED shaking, Danielle decided that she and Jake couldn't continue like this. It wasn't that she thought they should go back down; she knew from the summer that descending a slope is often far more difficult and dangerous than climbing it. She couldn't even imagine what descending a slippery, unstable mountainside would be like. And of course going down wouldn't solve their main problem in the first place. Yet neither could they just keep climbing in the way they'd been climbing. They couldn't keep taking their chances. They needed to proceed in a safer, more methodical, more powerful way.

Danielle had initially considered Jake's plan to improvise equipment as nothing more than a loony scheme. Mountaineering gear was highly sophisticated. Each piece of equipment had its own specialized purpose. Protection, for example: the various sorts of hardware that climbers use to safeguard themselves from falling. There were all sorts of gadgets and chunks of metal to fit the various kinds of cracks or protuberances in whatever cliff you were climbing. You had to use the right kind for the situation. Use the wrong kind and it might come loose. If matching the tool to the task was so important, then you couldn't just turn one tool into another. At least not without asking for big trouble.

But now Danielle started to see that the situation wasn't so simple. True, they had to match the tool to the task. The only problem was, they didn't have many tools—certainly not the tools they should have had with them. Yet they still had the task: climbing Mount Remington. Up till now she'd assumed they were better off just taking their chances. Improvising equipment had seemed riskier than climbing without any gear at all. Now she thought different. If they hadn't improvised a climbing rope out of Dad's towline, Danielle would have been dead already. So maybe Jake was right. Maybe they should try to figure out some way of protecting themselves after all.

The question was *how*. They had just a few dozen pieces of equipment, most of them ordinary tools. They had very little time. And of course the circumstances didn't allow them much leeway for trial and error. How could they succeed at the task facing them? Danielle didn't know. All she knew was that they had to try.

Danielle said, "All right, smartie—you want to improvise some gear? Great. Here's your chance."

Jake fidgeted, shifting his weight from one foot to the other, then back again. "I never said I *wanted* to," he replied. "Only that I thought we'd better."

"What's the difference? Either way we've got to do it." Danielle then picked up Jake's pack, unhitched the flap, and dumped its contents onto the rock they were sitting on. Soft things fell out first: woolen socks, a scarf, and the bag of leftover dog food. Then the empty thermos. Then everything else: a jumble of tools and gadgets. The whole mess clattered down between them. Two hammers. A chisel of some sort. A pair of pliers. Five or six screwdrivers. Flash's woven nylon leash. A coil of wire. All kinds of other stuff Danielle couldn't even identify. "Be my guest," she said.

Danielle thought Jake might give her a hard time, but he didn't. Almost before the tools had come to rest, he'd already started checking things out. Jake picked up a tool, examined it, picked up another, examined that one, picked up still another, examined it in turn, and soon worked his way through the entire heap. Danielle noticed that he'd also started sorting them: on the left, tools that pounded; on the right, tools that jabbed or poked; in the middle, everything else. Now and then he moved things around. Beyond the most obvious similarities and differences, however, she couldn't feel entirely sure what sort of patterns he saw here.

"How's it look?" she asked.

"Well, that depends on what you need."

"We need what climbers call protection. Gear that protects us from falling more than a few feet if we slip."

Danielle then explained to Jake what she had in mind. They wouldn't use any of these tools for the actual task of climbing; the climbing itself they'd do with their own hands and feet. Rather, they needed something to anchor into the cliff—something they could then pass the rope through. If the lead climber fell, the person below would tighten the rope so that the person above would fall only until the anchorpoint caught the rope. Of course that assumed the anchor didn't pull out. And the risk of the anchor pulling out was precisely why Danielle felt so nervous about this whole business of improvisation.

"So you want those spike-things climbers use?" Jake inquired. "What are they, Tetons?"

Danielle huffed at him. "Not Tetons—those are mountains in Wyoming. You mean pitons."

"Tetons, pitons, whatever."

"Climbers don't even use pitons much anymore.

There must be a dozen more sophisticated devices—"

"Forget sophistication, all right? Let's just do what we can."

"Screwdrivers seem the best bet," Danielle said.

"That's what I think, too," Jake said. He held up one for Danielle to see—a thick-shafted screwdriver with a yellow-and-black plastic handle.

Danielle took it from Jake. She grasped it, hefted it, stabbed it twice at the rock right in front of her. "It seems real strong."

"Steel alloy."

"You think it'll hold?"

"There's only one way to find out."

With those words, Jake reached down again, picked up one of Dad's hammers, then reached out to the cliff. He used the hammer's claw to scrape away some of the snow accumulating on the surface. Spotting a crack about a quarter of an inch wide, Jake inserted the screwdriver's tip as far as it would go. That wasn't more than an inch. Then, wielding the hammer, he pounded the screwdriver in till only the plastic handle and one inch of the shaft protruded.

Danielle watched Jake patiently while he worked. Once he finished, though, she couldn't hold back any longer. She reached out, grabbed the handle, and tugged on it as hard as possible. It didn't even budge. Danielle tried shoving it upward, then downward. She couldn't detect even the slightest movement.

"It worked!" she exclaimed.

"Didn't I tell you?" Jake said, clearly pleased.

"All right, you told me," said Danielle. "Now just explain how we'll pull this off. We have only six screwdrivers."

Jake shrugged. "Well, we'll just have to recycle."

"Recycle?"

"You'll go first," Jake told her, "just as you have all along. You'll climb the cliff, you'll pound in the screwdrivers, you'll keep going. Then you'll belay while I come up after you, right? And I'll pull out the screwdrivers on my way up and turn them over to you once I reach you. Then you can reuse them."

"You're brilliant!" Danielle exclaimed.

"Isn't that how the system works?"

"Almost exactly."

Then at once Danielle's excitement evaporated. She told him, "There's only one problem."

"Problem?"

"The rope."

"What about it?"

"We need to attach the rope to the screwdriver."

"Mm—good point."

"The screwdriver is no help unless it's attached to the rope."

Jake smiled abruptly. "I know, we can *wire* it on!"

Danielle couldn't believe what she was hearing. Jake still hadn't grasped even the most basic concepts. "Don't be ridiculous—the rope has to slide through. I'll be pounding these things into place while I climb. One after another. The rope follows me up. You'll be the belayer sitting below. Then, if I fall, you'll tighten the rope, I'll fall only just past the highest piece of protection, and we'll both be okay. But if the rope can't slide through, the system won't work."

"So how would you usually attach the rope to the protection?" Jake asked.

"With 'biners."

Jake's expression showed his bafflement. "What the hell are 'biners?" He must have thought she said *beaners*.

"Carabiners. Big metal clips. They look sort of like oval rings, only they have a hinged gate you can open and close. You hook them into the protection, then open the gate and clip in the rope."

Jake started poking through the heap of gear. "We sure don't have anything like that," he said gloomily.

They sat there a while. Danielle could sense her mood dropping almost by the second. What had felt like a breakthrough just a few minutes earlier now seemed a bad joke. She couldn't imagine how all these efforts would help them. They were wasting their time. They should just go ahead and take a chance, she decided. Either they'd make it or they wouldn't. If they fell, then at least death would be quick. It seemed impossible that they'd pull off what they were attempting.

At some point Danielle realized that the tension she felt had prompted her to fiddle with Flash's leash. She'd been twisting the thick nylon ribbon in her hands; by now it was a tangled mess. Danielle looked down at it. Loops of nylon . . . "They wouldn't have to be metal," she said suddenly.

"What wouldn't?" Jake asked.

"Carabiners."

"No—no, I guess they wouldn't."

At once Danielle lifted the tangled leash for Jake to see. "We could use loops of *this* stuff."

"Loops?"

"We'll cut lengths of Flash's leash—lengths maybe a foot long—and we'll tie one around each screwdriver's shaft."

"Sure, but how—"

"Like this." Danielle cut a length of the leash and looped it around the base of the screwdriver's shaft where it stuck out of the rock. "Wouldn't this work?" she asked.

Jake looked uncertain for a moment, then said, "I guess so."

"Would the leash be strong enough?"

Another pause. He seemed to be figuring out something. "It should be. That stuff is about a thousand-pound test—"

"I'm not *that* heavy," Danielle said, teasing him as her spirits started to soar again.

"But the big question," Jake went on, "would be the knot." He tugged the dangling ends of the nylon leash material, which fluttered slightly in the wind.

"The knot?"

"Well, you said we'd tie the loops around the rope. Obviously that means there'll be a knot."

"Yeah, you're right."

"Do you know a knot strong enough to hold?"

Danielle thought fast. At Mountain Mastery she'd learned a lot of ropecraft, including how to tie all kinds of knots. There was something called an Englishman's knot, a good way to splice two ropes. The Mountain Mastery instructors had used it to make loops of nylon webbing, too—what some of them called flat rope. And Flash's leash was a lot like flat rope. Danielle couldn't see any reason why that knot wouldn't work.

"I think we can do it," she said.

"So we have what we need?" Jake asked.

"I guess so."

They looked at each other for a moment.

Then, at almost exactly the same instant, each of them said, "So what are we waiting for?"

TWENTY-TWO
▲▲

THEY WORKED THEIR WAY OFF that rubble-strewn slope as carefully as possible. Once or twice Danielle and Jake almost started new rock slides. The mountain felt delicate, unstable, almost as treacherous as if it had been made of ice. Yet somehow they managed to get off the rubble. Once they'd reached a steeper but far more solid cliff a hundred feet higher up, Jake felt a sense of relief he'd never expected to feel in such a precarious place. If nothing else, he thought, at least Danielle would be able to use their improvised equipment.

"Okay," said Danielle, looking nervous, "here goes nothing."

"Good luck," Jake said.

She started up.

Watching from ten or fifteen feet below, Jake couldn't tell exactly what Danielle was doing. He could see her reaching for handholds, stepping for footholds, and shifting her position as she made each move. He could see her fumbling with the tools now loaded into her daypack, adjusted so she could wear it slung like a pouch below her left arm. He could see her swing back with the hammer and slam away at the screwdriver she was pounding in just then. He could see her standing there, trying to keep her balance, while tying lengths of Flash's leash onto the screwdriver. And he could see that all in all she was making good progress. But Jake couldn't really see enough to feel confident of what was happening. Danielle seemed to be taking too long. He got cold just standing there. Snow gathered on his coat, cap, gloves, and glasses. Jake couldn't shake the fear that they'd take so long getting up that the cold and snow would get the best of them.

This had all turned out much harder than he'd expected. It's a good thing he hadn't known *how* hard, Jake told himself, or he never would have tried climbing Mount Remington in the first place. But here they were. Near the top? He couldn't tell. The only thing Jake knew was that he was somewhere below his sister on a cliff so steep that they had to hook themselves into it to keep from falling.

Danielle's voice reached him from above: "Off belay."

"Belay off," Jake called back, more comfortable by now with the signals Danielle had taught him. Then he got ready to take his turn climbing. He dropped the rope, stepped away from the coil at his feet, and moved the coil slightly to one side. He lifted up his pack and put it on. He waited as Danielle pulled up the loose lengths of rope and prepared to assume the belayer's role.

"Belay on," she called down to him.

"Climbing," Jake called back.

"Climb."

He started up. The first few moves were always hard. Jake's muscles felt tired from such a long wait in the belay position; it took a while to stretch out and limber up. He reached overhead with his right hand. He groped about, hoping his gloved fingers could find a safe handhold. Then, once he'd found a protruding chunk of granite to grab, he raised his right boot, probed the rocks before him with the toe, and tried to locate a foothold. He could feel a crack of some sort to jab the toe in. After struggling to make it hold his weight, Jake decided to take a chance. It held. From there he could boost himself up nine or ten inches, maybe more, while reaching up first with the left hand, then with the left foot, till they found their own resting places. Jake repeated this sequence time after time, varying the moves according to what the cliff required, and gradually worked his way up-ward.

Little by little he climbed with more confidence.

The hard part wasn't really the physical exertion. It was finding the right placement for his hands and feet. Jake tried to find where Danielle had stepped— sometimes he could see her footprints in the snow— but that didn't always help. Danielle was so much bigger and stronger than Jake that she could reach farther and more easily than he could. Still, that wasn't all bad. Glancing upward, he could see her peering down from where she sat on an overhanging rock; the rope dangled, quivering, between them; and he felt a great sense of reassurance in knowing that she'd catch him if he fell.

Reassurance—and resentment. For although Jake felt delighted to have his sister looking after him like that, he felt frustrated at the same time to feel dependent on her. It confused him to feel both the reassurance and the resentment. It ought to be one way or the other, he told himself. His feelings shouldn't have been so contradictory. Yet they were. And in this strange situation, Jake couldn't do anything to simplify what he felt.

Now and then he stopped to pull out the protection that Danielle had put in while on her way up. Jake started by untying the loops of Flash's leash. Sometimes he could do that with his fingers; sometimes he had to pick the loops apart with the tip of his house key; sometimes he used his dad's pliers. The knots Danielle had tied were amazingly tough. Pulling them apart often took longer than Danielle had required for tying them in the first place.

Then, pocketing the length of leash, Jake would set to work on the screwdriver that the leash had been tied to. That was even trickier than untying the knots. First he'd tap the screwdriver lightly with his hammer. If it came loose right away from where it stuck out of the cliff, he'd feel both pleased and worried—pleased because the speed of removal had saved him a lot of work, worried because he started wondering how much security the screwdriver had provided in the first place. Would a loose screwdriver hold Danielle's weight in a fall? Probably not. Was it possible that this whole system of protection was nothing but a big joke? Maybe so.

Still, it seemed the best they could do. Jake wasn't about to suggest that they try something else. Even now they'd taken so long climbing Mount Remington that he worried constantly about Mom and Dad. A glance at his watch showed him the time. Ten minutes till two o'clock. There really wasn't any alternative to continuing upward.

Jake tugged repeatedly at the screwdriver he was working on. No go. He tapped it again with the hammer. It still wouldn't budge. Then he grasped it in his right hand, tilted it upward, pulled it downward, and repeated these motions several times, till at last he worked the shaft out. Jake reached over his left shoulder and dropped the screwdriver into the open pack. Almost at once he started up again.

The snow was what bothered him most. Without the snow, Jake told himself, this wouldn't be so bad. Steep, yes. Tricky, yes. But not so dangerous. The snow coming down all over the rocks made a risky situation much worse. Even the most ordinary move, such as taking a step from one stairlike rock to one slightly higher, was treacherous. Jake never felt sure of his footing. The rocks weren't icy—the snow settled down as lightly as dust—but it still made the cliff slippery. He couldn't trust anything underfoot. He felt as if he'd go shooting off the mountain without a moment's warning.

This is why Jake did what he could to clear the way ahead of him. He brushed off the powdery snow with his ski gloves. He used the claw-end of a hammer to scrape away some of the denser stuff that Danielle's boots had packed down on her way up. Sometimes he even jabbed at especially slick spots with a screwdriver. With the rock exposed, Jake could proceed more safely. Yet even so, he didn't feel safe there, he worried about each step he took, and he wondered how long they could keep going without an accident.

An accident . . .

It's not as if he couldn't remember what had happened; rather, it was that Jake tried *not* to remember it. How old had he been? Six, seven, eight? Probably about seven. Old enough, anyway, to feel he could look out for himself. Yet that summer, while on a vacation trip somewhere in Maine—

He recalled the other boys' dare: *Betcha can't swim out to the diving platform in the lake.*

He recalled the race down to the shore, the shouts, the wild splashing, the desperate effort as all the kids—boys and girls alike—clawed their way through the chilly water.

He recalled the fatigue, the cramps, the struggle for breath, the sudden mouthfuls of water—

"Jake!"

Jake broke through suddenly, gasping, as he reached the surface. He glanced about desperately. Rock and snow, not water, surrounded him now.

"Jake—what's taking you so long?"

He looked upward to Danielle above him. The sight of her shocked him, as if she'd popped up out of nowhere. Yet seeing her pleased him, too. She'd found a place to sit. Jake didn't quite understand how his sister had hooked herself into the cliff. He wasn't sure he *wanted* to know. All he could see was her feet dangling over the edge and, now and then, her face peering down at him when she glanced his way. All he could hope was that Danielle knew what she was doing.

"You okay?" she asked.

"Yeah—fine."

"You're just standing there."

"I'm trying to catch my breath."

"Okay. But I'm sort of worried about the time."

Jake started up again. Right hand first, then right foot. Left hand next, then left foot—

At just that moment he fell. As if he'd set his foot on a stair just as the stair collapsed, Jake felt a single rock simply drop away under his weight. Jake went down with it. Before he could yell, though, the rope caught him short. Jake's body jolted, slamming into the cliff. Things jabbed at his body: at his head, jaw, shoulder, hip. The pain was so intense that Jake felt stunned, almost paralyzed.

That was it. He'd made it to the platform. He'd done what the boys had dared him to do. But he was too exhausted, too badly chilled, to pull himself up. He'd inhaled some water; he'd panicked. He'd gone under once already and hadn't been able to catch a breath when he broke through. Then someone had caught hold of him. Someone was pulling him up. Coughing, choking, and gagging, Jake made it onto the platform. He felt relieved to be safe on the warm, dry wood. Relieved—until he heard the boys' snickers and realized who had saved him.

Later, his cousin Peter had taunted him: "You're such a wimp you had to be saved by your *sister!*"

Jake groped at the cliff, tried to find something to

139

grasp. He got hold of a rock in his left hand but lost his grip a moment later. Then he reached out again and caught hold of something bigger. At any moment he expected to plummet. Yet he took hold of the cliff so hard that nothing could have pried him loose. Then his boots managed to find a ledge or ridge of some sort and take hold there.

Only then did he realize how short a distance he'd fallen. One foot, two feet at most. Even if he let go of the cliff right now, he wouldn't have fallen farther. Danielle's grip on the rope held him fast.

Jake became aware of Danielle calling out to him: "Hey! Are you all right?"

At first he felt too scared to look. Surely the slightest movement would dislodge him. Then, carefully, Jake glanced upward.

Danielle was staring down at him. Her face showed worry and fear.

"I'm—I'm fine," he called back.

"You sure?"

"I'm just fine."

"Can you climb?"

Jake glanced at his own hands right before him. Even as he watched, snow began dusting the backs of his ski gloves. "Yes—yes, I can climb," Jake told her. "I can definitely climb."

TWENTY-THREE
▲▲

AND SO THEY CLIMBED. WITH Danielle climbing first while Jake belayed, then Jake catching up to her while Danielle belayed, they worked their way upward. Not fast, but carefully. This is what matters, Danielle kept reassuring herself. Slow but sure. Take your time. Whatever got them to the top alive would do the trick.

But the climb got harder, not easier. The cliff grew steeper. The rocks turned slicker. Handholds and footholds became more difficult to find and less reliable even once Danielle found them. She worked harder and harder to make her way upward, yet she felt less and less secure with every passing moment. She had trouble locating cracks to hold the screwdrivers, too, and the crusty snow accumulating there made the metal shafts hard to secure. Danielle couldn't help feeling that her hold on Mount Remington was so feeble now that even a gust of wind would blow her and Jake right off the peak.

The storm picked up again; snow started falling fast and thick. Soon Danielle could barely see Jake below.

"Hey!" she called out.

"Yo!" he shouted back.

"Still there, Jake?"

After a brief silence, his voice reached her again: "Who's Jake? I'm the Abominable Snowman!" But the words sounded shaky, and neither Jake nor Danielle laughed at them.

She waited for Jake to reach her. Once he did, settled in, and took the belay position again, Danielle started up without speaking. She felt too cold to talk.

The rocks grew even steeper, looser, more slippery. Now and then Danielle dislodged chunks of rock that plunged out of sight, knocking more chunks loose, till she worried that she'd bash her brother off the cliff and get yanked off, too, once Jake fell—that, or else the whole mountainside would crumble beneath them. At other times what slipped was Danielle herself: luckily not far, just a few inches when she lost her grip or footing, but far enough to frighten her. What had been her confidence and delight in the climb quickly deteriorated into doubt and dread.

Soon she noticed her hands becoming alternately achy and numb. Danielle flexed her fingers and felt them throb. Soon the throbbing stopped, though, which pleased her at first, then worried Danielle even more. Was this frostbite, she wondered? She'd heard about frostbite at Mountain Mastery, but never experienced it—even the Rocky Mountain summer nights, though chilly, weren't *that* cold. This was something else altogether. Were they already this close to freezing? What worried her was how much dexterity she'd already lost. Holding Dad's hammer in her right hand, Danielle could no longer feel confident that her fingers grasped it tightly.

Soon the tools seemed barely adequate: good enough, she decided, only to get them into deeper and deeper trouble. Jake and Danielle kept suffering small accidents. Once, while reaching for a handhold, Danielle slipped so abruptly that she couldn't catch herself. Luckily, she'd just finished anchoring another screwdriver and tying a loop of Flash's leash around the rope when Jake's quick grip on the rope caught her short. Danielle dropped no more than eighteen or twenty inches. The jolt hurt—but far less so than a longer fall would have. She fumbled about for a while, trying to get hold of the cliff again. She succeeded, though not fast enough to avoid imagining that all the carefully placed protection would fail, the rope would tear free, and both of them would tumble and slam their way down the mountainside.

Danielle couldn't shake the feeling that they

should have been doing more than they were. They should have been making better use of their tools. Never mind that they were improvising. Somehow they should have been trying something else—experimenting, expanding their range. The gambles they'd taken so far had worked, but Danielle wasn't sure their luck would hold. And if it didn't? Then they were probably stuck.

Yet what could they do? Danielle didn't know. Her lack of ideas scared her. They'd left Mom and Dad at seven, almost eight hours earlier. Even so, it wasn't just fear she felt but also embarrassment. Here she was, a far more experienced climber than Jake, yet she couldn't figure out what to do. The thought of failing at their task made Danielle ache even more than the wind and the snow did.

She kept going. Danielle told herself they had no choice. Jake depended on her. Not just Jake: Mom and Dad, too. How could she let them down? How could she allow herself to fail?

Danielle reached up with her gloved hand. The fingers groped for a place to anchor their tips. Yet the rock felt so slick that Danielle's hands just skittered around, never quite catching hold of anything. No matter how hard Danielle worked to grip the rocks, the rocks somehow refused to be gripped. Then she reached up with the hammer and bashed at the surface overhead. Snow and bits of ice rained down on her. She bashed harder and harder. More ice came down. To her dismay, Danielle realized that the slope she'd reached had become crusted with a layer of dense snow; the snow in turn glistened with a coating of ice.

"What's the problem?" Jake called up to her from eight or ten feet below.

"Ice," Danielle said almost absentmindedly.

"What?"

"Ice!" she shouted. Then, bashing at the rocks again and again, she yelled, "Ice! Ice! Ice! Ice!"

Danielle couldn't believe they'd get stuck now. They'd worked so hard. They'd been through so much. Mom and Dad needed their help so badly. Jake and Danielle needed to succeed for their own sake, too. Yet here they were, unable to proceed up a V-shaped gulley somewhere on the upper reaches of Mount Remington, all because of a little ice!

Danielle clawed desperately at the rocks before her. She got a foot or so farther up; then her hands and boots slipped simultaneously and she slid backward, crouching, helpless to slow her fall. Only at the last moment did she catch hold of some exposed rocks and manage to stop.

She clung there, panting. That was the worst slip yet. Another few feet and she would have toppled down onto Jake, knocking him loose as she fell.

She tried again, this time more carefully. Danielle

gained only nine or ten inches upward, then slipped. Once more she stopped right at the brink.

Clutching the rocks, Danielle started to cry. She wasn't crying in sadness but in anger. Anger that she couldn't get past this stupid, pointless obstacle in her path. Anger that she'd chosen a route so narrow there wasn't any alternate course either to the right or the left. Anger that no matter how strong she was, no matter how well she climbed, no matter how hard she tried, she couldn't think of any way to solve the problem.

That's what infuriated Danielle more than anything else. Years before, she'd heard one of her uncles talking with Dad while the two men watched Jake and Danielle playing. Jake had figured out how to make a tower out of rubber bands linking wooden rods together. Danielle, attempting to make her own castle, had failed. In frustration Danielle had broken her rods and stomped on the pieces.

"Well," said her uncle, "I guess we know which of them has the brawn and which has the brains." It had always been like that. Everyone thought Danielle was a witless jock.

In anger and exasperation, Danielle lifted her dad's hammer and smashed time after time, harder and harder, at the ice-coated rocks in front of her.

TWENTY-FOUR
▲▲

JAKE COULDN'T BELIEVE HOW hard the snow was coming down. It didn't even seem like snow—more like something you'd see if you looked through a microscope at some really foul pond water: tiny creatures trembling and quivering, swarming everywhere, shooting every which way at once. He wanted to find the sight amusing but didn't. It was too scary. The density of all that snow coming down was bad enough. Its effects were even worse. In just a few minutes Jake found his chest, hands, and face caked with snow. Everything else, too: the cliff before him. He could barely see what he was climbing.

Somehow he managed to fumble his way up to Danielle. She was sitting right at the base of two flat boulders that angled steeply upward in a way that formed a granite trench or chute. A lot of snow had accumulated there. He saw ice, too—undoubtedly the ice Danielle had been shouting about. Jake felt thrilled to reach his sister. He found it hard to believe they had much farther to go before reaching the top.

As soon as he got up, though, he knew something was wrong. Danielle sat there doubled up as if sick. "What's the matter?" he blurted. "Are you all right?"

When she turned to him, Jake saw she was crying.

"What is it?" he asked.

Danielle gestured helplessly. "We can't do this!" she shouted. "We just can't!"

"Danielle—"

"Don't you see?"

Jake felt confused. "See what?"

Danielle now hunched so far over that Jake couldn't even hear the words right. All he could figure out was, "—everything—"

"What do you mean, *everything?*"

"Everything! The accident. Mom and Dad getting hurt. You and me trying to help them. Everything!"

Jake's confusion turned quickly to fear.

"We've been kidding ourselves," Danielle said.

"But don't you think—" Jake couldn't finish.

"I can't climb any more," Danielle told him. "I'm so tired. I'm just all tired out. My hands—" She held them out to him, the fingers pointing up, and flexed them slowly. "I can't move them very well."

"Here," Jake said, reaching out to her, taking her

hands in his own, and rubbing them. "I'll warm you up."

"No—"

"Let me help you—"

"No, it's not just that." Danielle motioned again toward the boulders.

"What is it?" he asked. He felt more and more alarmed as he watched her and listened to her.

"Ice," Danielle said. That one little word seemed to carry all the world's despair and pain.

Jake looked over Danielle's shoulder and saw what she meant. The granite trench before them shone with an irregular glaze. Why here? Jake had no idea. All he knew was that when he reached out to touch it, this rock slab felt far more slippery than anything they'd seen so far on the climb.

He didn't know what to say. "We'll make it," he told Danielle, yet the words didn't sound convincing even to his own ears. "I'm sure we'll make it."

Just then Danielle leaned over, took hold of Jake by the arms, and shoved her face against his chest. "I'm sorry!" she blurted. "I'm so sorry!"

Jake told her, "Don't cry. We'll think of something."

"But *what!*" Danielle shouted, accusing more than asking him.

"The screwdrivers."

"I tried that. They won't hold—the cracks are too tiny and slippery."

149

Jake thought fast. "Chisels. Nails. Something sharp."

"The chisels didn't work, either," Danielle said. "We don't have any nails."

"Wire?" he ventured.

Danielle stopped crying long enough to laugh a sputtery laugh. "What would we do with *wire!*"

Jake sat back, stumped. He wasn't offended so much as scared. What could they do that would get them out of there? He couldn't even guess. He felt too cold to think. No matter how hard he tried, Jake couldn't come up with a single idea. Maybe his mind was freezing.

He wanted to reassure Danielle. He wanted to hug her and hold her and convince her that everything would be fine. He hugged her and patted her on the back, but almost at once he started crying, too, for he couldn't think of anything to say. Maybe things *wouldn't* be fine, Jake thought. Maybe things *wouldn't* turn out all right. Maybe they'd done everything they could but had still lost the gamble. After a while he managed to say, "I'm sorry, too."

They held each other for a long time. It wouldn't help much, Jake told himself. The two of them couldn't hold off the cold much longer than they'd hold it off alone. Still, it seemed right to try. They didn't have much heat to share, but somehow the chill wasn't quite so bad that way.

He'd heard stories about people freezing to death.

Supposedly it didn't hurt much. You just sort of fell asleep and never woke up. Even now he could feel himself getting drowsier and drowsier. At some point, though, rousing for a moment, Jake looked up. He forced his eyes open. He was still snuggled against his sister, but she had twisted enough to one side that she could face the boulders.

Danielle was bashing at the rock with Dad's hammer. With each blow, chips of icy snow flew like sparks. Some of the chips sprayed toward Jake; a few even struck his face. He held out his hand, motioning for her to stop. Before he could speak, however, something caught his attention.

Danielle wasn't bashing at the rock just to let off her frustration. She was experimenting. She was trying to figure something out.

The hammer came down once, twice, three times.

Chips flew outward.

Then, without saying a word, Danielle turned the hammer around. She continued to grip its metal shaft by the rubber-clad handle, but now she struck at the icy granite with the claw, not with the head. The claw was the side you used for pulling nails out— a curved, pointed piece of forged steel.

"What are you doing?" Jake asked.

Danielle replied, "Improvising."

Jake watched in puzzlement. Then, suddenly, he understood. "An ice ax?"

"You got it." Danielle struck the slab several times with the hammer's claw. Instead of scattering lots of chips, it sent fewer of them outward and mostly sideways; otherwise the metal dug deep into the crust. "The claw cuts in much more steeply than a regular ice ax would," she told Jake. "It's more like what climbers use for what they call vertical ice. It's not very sharp." She pulled the hammer back with her right hand, then stroked the claw with the fingers of her right. "But like you said—beggars can't be choosers."

Jake felt a surge of hope and delight. "You think it'll work?"

"There's only one way to find out." She reached out to Jake. "Here," she said. "I'll need your hammer, too."

He handed it over at once.

TWENTY-FIVE

▲▲

THE HAMMERS WORKED, DANielle told herself. Just as the screwdrivers functioned as crude pitons and the loops of nylon leash served as crude carabiners, the hammers worked well as crude ice axes. She couldn't quite believe it, but they worked just fine.

Something else she couldn't believe: Danielle herself had thought up half the system. Not Jake. Danielle. Even though Jake suggested the general idea of improvising hardware, Danielle was the one who figured out most of the specifics. First the fake carabiners, now the fake ice axes. And the system worked!

No wonder Jake got such a kick out of doing this, she told herself. It wasn't just coming up with a new idea. It was getting in a jam, then finding a way out. It was a great feeling—a feeling much like what she'd felt at

Mountain Mastery when, stuck high on a cliff, Danielle had taken a chance, pulled herself out of danger, and discovered strength she hadn't even known she had.

TWENTY-SIX

▲▲

SOMEHOW HE'D DONE IT, JAKE thought. He'd fallen, yet he'd pulled himself up. He'd kept going. He'd overcome the pain, the fear, the doubt that he could continue. Despite dropping two or three feet and slamming into the cliff, despite banging his shoulder and his face, he hadn't given up. Here he was now, heading up all over again.

For the first time, Jake started to understand why Danielle liked sports so much. Not because of winning—coming out ahead of everyone else. Instead, because of coming out ahead of *himself.*

He glanced at his watch. Three-thirty.

Now the biggest challenge rose right before them.

"Belay on?" Danielle called down to Jake.

"On belay," he shouted back.

"Climbing."

"Climb."

TWENTY-SEVEN

▲▲

CLIMBING THAT ICY TRENCH was the hardest work Danielle had ever done. With a hammer in each hand, she struck out with the right one till it caught securely, then flexed her biceps to pull her body upward while she kicked at the slab with her boots, struggling to find some kind of foothold. Then she struck out with the left hammer and, kicking once again, pulled herself still higher. More often than not, her feet skittered around, helplessly at first. Two or three efforts let her find rough spots for the boot soles to catch on; the slab's angle was sufficiently gradual that she could get by with risky footholds. Somehow she kept going.

Danielle proceeded by exerting most of her weight on the hammers. Sometimes she felt the claws slipping, and once or twice she almost lost control. Yet she managed to keep her grip anyway. She pulled herself upward a few inches at a time. Panting, gasping, and fighting the fatigue that left her close to passing out, Danielle managed to fumble up the trench all the way to the top.

Then it was Jake's turn. Danielle didn't even stop to rest. She tied a length of Flash's nylon leash onto one of the two hammers and lowered it to Jake. After Jake untied it, Danielle pulled up the leash, tied on the second hammer, and lowered it as well. Then she assumed the belay position, told Jake what to do, and coaxed him all the way up.

The snowstorm had eased again. Snow still sifted down from above but so much more thinly now that it might as well have stopped altogether. Danielle could see the snow-covered rocks around them, the clouds massing around the mountain, and even some of the land visible below the clouds. She could see that they were on a mountain; she could also see the contours of that particular peak. But where she expected to see the cliff above her, she saw only a low mound of snowy granite rising off to the left. Mount Remington didn't keep going higher, higher, and higher. On the contrary: it seemed to be leveling off.

Danielle felt the angle of the slope underfoot starting to ease. The mountain felt less and less steep. With each step the ground seemed more nearly level.

Soon Danielle and Jake couldn't even keep going on all fours—they had to stand upright. Thick mist streaked around them, so they couldn't see much of the terrain, but within a few minutes they weren't climbing at all; they were just walking over an uneven but relatively flat surface.

"Danielle," said Jake, badly winded. "Danielle—" He stopped, leaned over, coughed, then stood upright again, heaving for breath. "I think we—I think this is—"

"The top!" Danielle exclaimed. She wanted to say more but couldn't. She wanted to shout, to scream for joy, to thank her brother for teaming up to do what they'd done—but she couldn't. She could scarcely breathe, much less talk. All she could say was, "The— *top!*"

The snowfall had stopped. Great clouds massed below them, around them, almost everywhere but above them. They were so high up now that the only vistas Danielle could remember like this were what she'd seen from airplanes. Danielle suddenly understood what people meant by a breathtaking view.

Then, abruptly, she didn't care about the view at all. She didn't care if it was beautiful or ugly. She started looking around in a different, almost desperate way.

Something was wrong. Something about the view. Something that wasn't what she saw but was what she *didn't* see.

There was no weather station in sight.

Together Jake and Danielle worked their way over the jumble of rocks. They walked about fifteen or twenty feet ahead to where the flat place they'd reached began curving downward again. Clouds swept all around them. They couldn't see very far—perhaps a few dozen yards down the mountain. But that was just the problem. They were looking down the mountain. Down the mountain's far side.

Danielle turned, took twenty paces to the right, then turned again and worked her way to Jake's left. She peered over the edge and saw nothing but rock and snow vanishing into the clouds below. The sight chilled her more than the wind needling at her.

Danielle watched her brother doing what she herself had just finished doing, except that Jake went farther and peered still more intently over the edge. They must have missed something, she told herself. They hadn't looked hard enough.

Yet she couldn't see anything like what they were looking for. There was nothing at all like a weather station.

They were at the summit.

Alone.

"We're dead," Danielle moaned. "Jake—we're dead."

TWENTY-EIGHT

▲▲

JAKE STUMBLED OVER TO HER. He had begun to shake and now shook so hard he couldn't stop. He couldn't believe all their efforts had come to this. He couldn't believe his plan hadn't worked. There was supposed to be a weather station up here. He'd seen it on TV. It had to be here. Yet the place around them looked as desolate as the moon. So Jake stood staring at his sister, at how miserable she looked with her gloved hands up against her mouth while she cried, and he felt hollow and terrible inside. "Danielle," he said. "I'm sorry—" A moment later he started crying, too. He reached out to embrace her.

They held each other a long time. He wanted to re-assure Danielle, to suggest a new idea that would save them after all, but he couldn't think of anything. All he could think about was the cold. What would it feel like, freezing to death? How long would it take? Would it be peaceful, as some people said it was? Peaceful! What a joke! How could it be peaceful? Even if Jake went numb and didn't feel the pain of his fingers and toes turning to ice, of his blood thickening to slush, then surely he'd still think every last second about how he'd let down Mom, Dad, and Danielle—

She was pushing him away. That push hurt worst of all, and tears filled Jake's eyes so fast that his vision went blurry.

"This is *your* fault!" she screamed.

"Danielle, I'm sorry—"

"*Your* fault!"

"Listen—"

"You and your stupid weather station!"

"Danielle, listen—"

She took him by the shoulders and shook him.

"I'm sorry," Jake shouted back. "I'm sorry, I'm sorry, I'm sorry!"

She shook him harder and harder. She shook him so hard that Danielle almost knocked him over. But then, gradually at first, the way she shook him started to change. She wasn't punishing him now— she was trying to get his attention. Puzzled at first, Jake soon understood what his sister was doing. He pulled back from her. He wiped his eyes with the back of his glove.

"*Look!*" she cried. "Just look!"

Danielle was pointing into the clouds sweeping past from left to right.

"What is it?"

"Over there!"

Jake leaned this way and that to get a better look. At first all he saw was the soft gray-white nothingness of the clouds. Then, looking more closely, he realized that what he saw wasn't just the clouds; it was also the clouds shifting, parting, and revealing something beyond. First just textures, then shapes. Some sort of low horizontal box. Some vertical lines. He couldn't tell what it was. Something inside the clouds?

At that moment the clouds shifted and whatever he'd been seeing took on more detail. Walls. Windows. A metal roof. Some sort of shed next to the main structure. A big antenna poking up from the shed. A satellite dish mounted on the roof. The longer he looked, the more he saw. And he saw something else, too: a stony ridge that connected Danielle and Jake's summit to another summit, a pile of massive boulders topped by these ghostly buildings.

"The weather station!" Jake exclaimed.

"We're on a false summit," Danielle said. "That's the real summit over there."

Without another word they rushed over to the edge, and, scrambling as fast as possible without tumbling headfirst, they climbed down toward the ridge connecting where they were to where they wanted to be.

TWENTY-NINE

▲▲

DANIELLE WAS SHAKING HARD by the time she and Jake worked their way over to the weather station. Her hands shook, her knees shook, her whole body shook. She was shaking from excitement but mostly from the cold. Danielle couldn't remember having ever felt so cold. She almost felt as if she were bleeding to death, except that her blood was heat, and all the heat was leaking from her body. In a few minutes the heat would be gone.

Danielle and Jake staggered the last few feet up the slope to the weather station. Drifts lay piled on the far side of the buildings, drifts so deep that Danielle had to wallow to get anywhere. She lost her balance several times trying to push through. Twice she fell over and ended up with a faceful of snow. Yet somehow she managed, and Jake did, too, and they made it all the way to the biggest of the buildings.

"Where's the door?" Danielle asked.

"Maybe this way," Jake answered, and they worked their way around to the right.

Danielle started pounding on the door the moment she reached it. Her hands felt so numb, however, that she couldn't even make a fist. She wasn't really pounding, she was slapping. Then Jake started in, too, striking the door as hard as he could.

They both stopped and fell silent.

All they heard was the whistle of the wind and the fluttering noise it made against the weather station.

"Maybe nobody's home," Jake said.

"Don't be ridiculous," Danielle told him, but his words chilled her even more than the cold. Was it possible? Could they have come all the way here only to reach a vacant building?

She glanced around. There was a relatively flat, open area right next to the building—the sort of area someone might use to park a truck up here—but no truck in sight. Danielle saw no vehicles at all. On the other side of this area, though, was a shedlike structure, and she decided that must be a garage. But she didn't really care. She knew someone was up here. Someone *had* to be up here.

Danielle started pounding again.

Jake interrupted her: "Listen!"

She held off. She waited.

Just then she heard something. "Music!" Danielle exclaimed. Some kind of jazz.

At once she went back to pounding. "Open!" she yelled. "Open up! Please! We need help!"

Jake pounded, too.

Then they stopped, waited, listened.

Nothing happened.

Danielle could feel her excitement vanish in a moment's time. Surely they wouldn't climb all day only to discover that no one could hear them!

Before she could start pounding again, though, Jake said, "Wait—maybe the music's too loud." He took off his pack, pulled it open, and rummaged around inside. When he couldn't find what he wanted, he dumped everything out onto the snow.

"What are you doing?" Danielle asked.

Jake picked up Dad's biggest hammer. He said, "Improvising." At once he started banging on the door—banging so hard that each blow dented the metal.

The music stopped a few moments later.

Danielle could almost imagine that she heard a voice.

Then Jake said, "Okay, get ready."

"Ready?" Danielle asked, unsure of what he meant. Watching, she saw Jake reach down to his empty pack. Just then Danielle saw what he was going to do, but she understood too late to stop him.

As the door swung open, revealing two startled men on the other side, Jake held out his empty pack like a Halloween bag.

"Trick or treat!"

THIRTY

▲▲

THE NEXT FEW MINUTES WERE so confusing that Jake couldn't follow everything that happened. The two men at the door stared at Jake and Danielle for a long moment, their expressions showing a mix of shock and amazement; then the men pulled Danielle and Jake inside the weather station and slammed the door. Jake was so unsteady by then that he slumped to his knees. One of the men helped him up while the other ran off shouting. When a third man showed up with the second, all three started asking loud questions, and both Jake and Danielle shouted answers back simultaneously. Jake felt dizzy from so much noise and motion. Dizzy—and tired. All he wanted was to lie down, fall asleep, and sleep forever.

In the midst of so much confusion, though, he felt sure of at least one thing. This weather station was the perfect place. Nowhere on earth had ever been so wonderful as this. The warmth alone brought tears to his eyes. That there could be a place where the snow and the wind never reached! And the light: thick, honey-colored light from all sorts of lamps. It didn't matter that the room these men now led them to looked like a lab, with low tables full of equipment along two sides and several computers set up at the far end. Jake looked around and felt sure that even a beach in Tahiti couldn't have been more of a paradise.

The men bustled about, trying to make Danielle and Jake more comfortable. They took off the teenagers' coats, made them sit on chairs, and wrapped them in big fluffy sleeping bags. One of the three—a short man with a full brown beard—left through a doorway. The second man, the tallest of the three, worked to pull off Jake's snow-encrusted boots. The third, who was huge and bald and dressed in a navy blue jogging suit, barraged Danielle with questions.

Jake could hear Danielle answering, but he couldn't follow everything she said. She spoke so fast that the words just rushed forth, tumbling and billowing, a blizzard of words. "So we decided to climb the mountain, only we didn't have the right gear, we had to fake it, we improvised, we did whatever we could, but we didn't really know if that would work—if we'd ever make it—and we didn't even know if you'd be up here anyway, we just *hoped* you would, and it was so, so scary not knowing—" Her voice faltered. "We just didn't know—we thought maybe we'd get up here and nobody would be here—" Her mouth kept moving but no words came out, and Jake could see his sister's eyes welling up.

The big man in the jogging suit watched Danielle a moment, then reached out to her with his huge arms. She leaned close to him and cried hard with her head pushed up against his shoulder. "It's okay," he told her. "You're safe. You both made it. We'll take good care of you."

Jake looked over just then and saw that the bearded man was reaching out to him with a mug. Steam rose from the mug. The man held another mug in his other hand. Cocoa? Coffee? When Jake took the mug he'd been offered, he saw that the liquid there wasn't brown but orange instead. "What is it?" he mumbled, his face still so numb that he couldn't say the words right.

"Orange juice," said the bearded man.

"*Hot* orange juice?"

"It'll warm you up. There's nothing better."

Jake had never drunk hot orange juice before, and it sounded kind of weird, but he was still so cold that he would have drunk almost anything hot. He took the mug, he raised it to his lips, he took a drink. At once he sputtered—the juice burned his tongue! But when he slowed down enough to get a careful sip, Jake couldn't believe how good it was. Not just the taste, which was fine. What thrilled him was how it *felt*. The orange juice slid down his throat spreading such a deep sense of well-being that the juice seemed more like light than liquid—pure, yellow light that seeped into his flesh and left him aglow. Jake wouldn't have been surprised if he'd looked down to find his chest and belly, his arms and legs, his hands and feet all radiant.

After that it was only a short while before the meteorologists radioed for help. Jake sat there, listening, not entirely sure what was happening yet aware that what he heard now added to his satisfaction.

". . . and report two stranded motorists," the tall man was saying into a microphone, "near the summit of Sluice Creek Pass. Over."

A staticky, garbled voice replied, but Jake couldn't understand all the words. He thought he heard someone ask, "How do you know?"

The tall man spoke at once: "Because two kids came up here to tell us. Over."

More garbled words: " . . . say . . . kids . . . ?"

"Kids," said the tall man. "Teenagers. Over."

There was a long period of static. Then, without any interruption, the voice said, "Please verify your last transmission. Did you say *teenagers*? Over."

"Affirmative. Teenagers—a boy and a girl. They

climbed Mount Remington to tell us about their parents. And now we're telling you. So could you please get a rescue organized? Over."

And for the first time, without any doubt or fear, Jake realized what he'd done. What he and Danielle had done. Jake turned to her just then and found his sister staring at him. Smiling.

THREE DAYS LATER...

▲▲▲

FROM THE SEVENTH-FLOOR VISI-
tors' lounge at Denver General Hospital, Danielle
could look out over the city and see all the way to the
mountains. Some of Denver's suburbs sprawled to
the west, dipping gradually in the low areas where the
South Platte River ran. Then the land rose again toward the foothills—first gradually, then more steeply—
until it tilted to become the Rockies beyond. She could
even see Mount Remington. It was pure white.

Danielle found it hard to believe that any of the
past few days' events had really happened. The drive
up. The accident. The long night in the car. The
climb. Reaching the summit. Everything about the
whole ordeal now seemed unreal, dreamlike. Even
the rescue did—the rescue most of all. Hearing the
meteorologists radio for help. Realizing that a heli-
copter was heading off to find Mom and Dad. Won-

dering if the copter would find them in time. Riding the meteorologists' Sno-Cat down the far side of Mount Remington—the side with a road. Driving back to Denver in the ambulance. Meeting up with Mom and Dad—safe!—at the hospital.

All of this seemed especially bizarre to Danielle because the scene around her now was so unlike anything that had happened earlier. The cityscape she saw from the hospital looked comfortable, almost summery. The sky was a cloudless blue. The trees had scarcely started changing colors. Not a patch of snow lay on the ground.

Yet Danielle knew everything had happened. She trusted her memory. Even if she'd forgotten, her hands would have reminded her: the bandages on several fingers and the ache of the frostbite beneath.

"Howdy, pardner."

Danielle turned to find Jake walking toward her in the visitors' lounge. "Hi," Danielle said, pleased to see him.

Dressed in a hospital gown and a terry cloth bathrobe, Jake looked pretty much the same as other teenage patients on the ward. In one respect, however, he looked altogether different. He wore one of those plastic penholders in the bathrobe pocket—the kind that nerds at school used to keep six or eight pens from staining their shirts. Danielle thought he looked totally ridiculous. Who but Jake would keep all those pens in his hospital bathrobe! She felt a sudden impulse to tease her brother. Something held her back, though. The rest of Jake's appearance restrained the urge to tease: his badly bruised face, the dressing on the left side of his jaw, and especially the mittenlike bandages covering both of his hands.

"How's it going?" Jake asked.

"Pretty good, pretty good," Danielle replied. "You?"

"Not bad."

"Hands are okay?"

"Better. Getting there."

They fell silent for a while. Both of them stared out the window past the city to the mountains.

Then, abruptly, Danielle asked, "Did you see *this?*" She picked up a newspaper from the chair beside him and handed it to Jake.

TEENS RESCUE SNOWBOUND MOM, DAD

Denver, Oct. 10. In the aftermath of a high-country auto accident, two Denver teenagers rescued themselves and their parents by seeking help from meteorologists atop snow-ravaged Mount Remington. Danielle Darcy, 14, and her brother, Jake, 13, climbed the Front Range peak during Saturday's blizzard. Despite minimal experience and equipment, the pair succeeded in reaching the peak's 14,060-foot summit and notified a crew on duty at the weather station located there. . . .

"This is great!" Jake exclaimed.

Danielle smiled as she watched her brother reading.

"When we go see Mom and Dad," Jake said, "let's take this and show them."

"Great idea."

"When will the nurses let us in?" Jake asked.

"I figure pretty soon."

"Have you talked with the doctors?"

"Just the intern. We'll see the other two once we're all in there together."

"What did the intern say?" Jake asked.

"Nothing we didn't hear when they spoke with Mom and Dad last time."

This didn't altogether satisfy Jake's curiosity, yet like Danielle herself, he seemed at least somewhat reassured. Mom and Dad were no worse. Dad's condition was stable—he had broken four ribs and cracked his breastbone—but the doctors seemed confident that the damage wasn't serious. Dad could probably go home within a few days and back to work in a month or so. Mom's situation was more problematic. One of her knees had suffered enough damage to require reconstructive surgery; the other was in better shape but would need extensive physical therapy. She'd be hospitalized for weeks. After that, they'd just have to see.

"Have you visited them yet?" Jake asked.

"Not since we were in there yesterday. Visiting hours start pretty soon, though." Before Jake could say anything further, Danielle went on: "You know, in some ways I think we've got the hard part still ahead of us."

"I know that."

"Even when Aunt Jenny and Uncle Pete get here, things'll be difficult for quite a while."

"I know."

"Maybe even *more* difficult—"

"Look," Jake said, "you don't have to lecture me."

"All right—sorry."

"We'll just do what we have to." Jake made an impatient gesture. "If we can climb Mount Remington together, we can do anything. We can certainly get through the next few months."

"Right." Smiling, Jake gazed at the newspaper still faceup on his lap. "Now maybe we should head over to the ortho ward." He stood carefully. When he tried to pick up the newspaper with his gauze-mittened hands, however, he couldn't.

Danielle helped him.

"Thanks, pal," he told her.

Danielle gazed out the window a few moments longer. In the late morning sun, the Front Range of the Rockies now looked almost too radiant for her eyes to tolerate. Partly visible behind one of the closer peaks, Mount Remington rose into a cloudless sky. It looked impossibly distant yet so clear that Danielle could almost imagine reaching out to touch it.

She stared a while, turned away from the window, walked down the corridor, and caught up with Jake where he was waiting for her. Then, together, they headed off to visit their parents.